"Let's dance,"

Johnny said, his voice soft.

"I don't want—"

She felt his lips move across the top of her head, and shivered. My God, was the scalp an errogenous zone? She'd never heard that it was, but hers was sure reacting like one.

He moved one arm down, and the next thing she knew his hand was snaking between their bodies and cupping her left breast.

"Cut it out," she warned him.

"And that was my best move in high school."

"We're not in high school, Johnny."

The next thing that happened was that his hands went to her waist and she was suddenly lifted until they were eye-level. "Put me down," she demanded. Instead of dropping her, he let her slowly slide down the length of his body, and the sensation was similar to riding a roller coaster. This time she felt like ordering him to do it again....

Dear Reader,

When two people fall in love, the world is suddenly new and exciting, and it's that same excitement we bring to you in Silhouette Intimate Moments. These are stories with scope and grandeur. The characters lead lives we all dream of, and everything they do reflects the wonder of being in love.

Longer and more sensuous than most romances, Silhouette Intimate Moments novels take you away from everyday life and let you share the magic of love. Adventure, glamour, drama, even suspense—these are the passwords that let you into a world where love has a power beyond the ordinary, where the best authors in the field today create stories of love and commitment that will stay with you always.

In coming months look for novels by your favorite authors: Linda Howard, Heather Graham Pozzessere, Emilie Richards and Kathleen Korbel, to name just a few. And whenever you buy books, look for all the Silhouette Intimate Moments, love stories *for* today's woman *by* today's woman.

Leslie J. Wainger
Senior Editor and Editorial Coordinator

Corrupted
BEVERLY SOMMERS

Silhouette Intimate Moments

Published by Silhouette Books New York

America's Publisher of Contemporary Romance

SILHOUETTE BOOKS
300 East 42nd St., New York, N.Y. 10017

ISBN: 0-373-07333-X

First Silhouette Books printing May 1990

Printed in the U.S.A.

BEVERLY SOMMERS

grew up in Evanston, Illinois, and went on to college in California, graduating with a major in English. Subsequently she has studied law, taught fifth grade, been a counselor in Juvenile Hall and owned an art gallery. She has lived in Spain and Greece, and currently makes her home in Northern California.

Chapter 1

Go home and pack a bag, you're going on special detail," said Lieutenant Wainger, something in his frosty gray eyes warning Sandy not to give him an argument.

Sandy shifted her weight onto her left leg and eyed him warily. "For how long?"

The lieutenant's eyes moved to the papers on his desk, giving her the idea they were already being dismissed.

Sandy persisted. "Who's going to feed my animals?"

Her partner nudged her. "Maybe my brother would feed them for you."

Sandy hadn't even known Chance had a brother. "They need more than food," she said. "They need attention." It was as much an answer to Chance as to get a reaction from the lieutenant.

The lieutenant cleared his throat in what sounded like a growl. "Are you a cop or a veterinarian, McGee?"

"Pets are just as much responsibility as children," she said. When that got not the slightest bit of attention, she asked, "Can I at least know how long I'm packing for?"

Lieutenant Wainger gave her a hard look. "Ten days."

"Ten days?"

"Incommunicado?" asked Chance.

The lieutenant sighed and made sure they heard it. His sighs were notorious as precursors of his temper. His voice was tightly controlled when he said, "You'll be briefed when you get back. Now get out of here and start packing."

"How long do we have?" asked Sandy.

"Less time than you had a minute ago," said the lieutenant. "I want the two of you back here by noon."

Sandy looked at her watch and then opened her mouth to argue, but Chance grabbed her arm and propelled her out of the lieutenant's office. "I don't know what you're complaining about," he said to her once they were outside and she had shaken free of his grip. "You've been doing nothing but talking about how bored you've been lately."

"It's going to be a stake-out," said Sandy.

"You don't know that."

"We're probably going to be stuck in a van without air-conditioning in some godforsaken locale. You can bet we're not getting an interesting assignment."

"Now me, I'm an optimist," said Chance. "I figure we're going on special duty to guard the stars of that movie they're filming in town, and they'll put us up in a luxury hotel, you know what I'm talking about?" He waited for an answer that didn't come. Sandy had gotten used to his rhetorical questions and waited them out. He kept eyeing her and finally said, "Bring a dress, I'll take you dancing."

"Fat chance," she said. "It's a stake-out, I'll bet on it."

"Bet you five bucks," said Chance, holding out his hand.

Sandy shook it. "You're on."

Still holding on to her hand he leaned down to her, his dark eyes gleaming, one of his black curls falling artfully over his forehead, his thick mustache framed by dimples practically twitching above the devastating grin on his face, and said, sotto voce, "You're hoping you'll lose, aren't you? Bring a sexy dress, just in case."

"You wish, Madrigal," muttered Sandy, yanking her hand out of his grasp before ducking around him and heading for the door to the parking lot. He might be a hero around the department, but he hadn't yet proved himself as anything but another macho cop to her.

Sandy took the mail out of her mailbox and let herself into her house. Fidel, her small, fluffy dog with the big feet, was already falling over himself trying to get to her. When she'd gotten him as a puppy from the pound, she had thought his big paws portended a large watchdog who would protect the house from bur-

glars. Instead, he'd grown up to be small and cow-
ardly, with oversized feet and a friendly propensity for
strangers.

The air conditioner was on low, but it was hot and
stuffy in the cottage, with the sun streaming through
the closed windows. Jackson, her large black cat, was
stretched out in the sunlight that was coming through
the sliding glass doors. He barely managed one half-
opened eye at her entrance.

Sandy gave her mail a cursory glance: the electric
bill, which could wait, a sales brochure from Burdine's, and a hurricane tracking chart. It was that time
of year again. She put them all in her desk and went
out to the kitchen and poured herself a glass of iced tea
from the pitcher in the refrigerator. She gulped half a
glass down before reaching for the wall phone and
calling Annie.

Luckily she was in her office. "What's up?" Anne
asked her.

"I've got a favor to ask. Would you feed my animals for me?"

"Sure."

"I hate to ask, with you and Jack still kind of honeymooning...."

"No problem."

"It's just with Bolivia in Beirut, and I don't really
know my neighbors that well..."

"Sandy, I'd be glad to feed them. I'll even take the
dog out."

"You wouldn't mind?"

"Listen, some day you can repay me by baby-
sitting."

Sandy caught her breath. "You're *pregnant*?"

"No, I'm not pregnant, but it's not totally inconceivable that someday I might be. So what's up, is it work or a vacation?"

"Some special assignment for ten days. With my luck, it'll be a stakeout."

"Well, give me a call if you can, let me know how it goes."

"I really hate to ask you to do this—"

"Will you quit it, Sandy? I don't mind feeding your animals."

"I'll leave the food out on the counter and a note on what to give them."

"Relax. Enjoy yourself. Will Chance be on the assignment, too?"

"Yes."

"Good. Maybe something will develop."

"I don't know if I want it to."

"He's sure not bad to look at."

"No, and he knows it. And he's always coming on to me. I think he might be a little too knowledgeable for me."

"Knowledge isn't a bad thing in a man, Sandy."

"I don't know, Annie. All the men think he's great, and most of the women, but he makes me nervous sometimes."

"That's called sexual tension."

"You sound like Chance. According to him, everything is related to sex in some way."

Anne chuckled. "Maybe he's right."

"You didn't talk like that before you were married."

"True."

"Not to change the subject, but have you heard from Bolivia?"

"Not even a postcard. What about you?"

"Nothing," said Sandy. "But that's Bolivia."

"I hate to think of her over there. I keep thinking she's going to be the next hostage."

"I'll bet she loves it."

Anne laughed. "I'll bet she does, too. And it doesn't hurt that Tooley's over there with her."

"Listen, Annie, I've got to go. I have to pack and be back for the briefing at noon."

"Take care of yourself, Sandy, and don't worry about the beasts. I'll take good care of them."

Sandy hung up the phone and went to look over her wardrobe. She didn't think she'd find anything that hadn't been there the last time she looked, but she could hope.

Chance made the call from a telephone booth while getting his Mustang gassed up. Ninety-nine in the shade and it had to be a hundred and ten in the phone enclosure. He could feel the pool of sweat building under his belt and trickling down into his pants. His shirt felt like it was stuck to his back with glue.

"It's me. Madrigal," he said, after he was put through.

"What's up?"

"I'll be on special assignment for a few days."

"Yeah? Well, keep in touch."

"That's just it, I might not be able to, you know what I mean?"

There was a pause then, "Anything we should know about?"

"I don't know. We haven't been briefed yet."

"Well, if it is—"

"I'll try."

"Undercover going undercover. There's a certain irony to that."

"Yeah, I guess," said Chance, but the connection had already been broken.

He pulled his shirt away from his chest and tried to let some air in to cool himself off. The air was as wet as he was, though, and offered no relief.

He'd swing by his folks' house, see if his mom had done his laundry yet. He'd need a few clean shirts, a couple pairs of slacks, maybe a sport jacket if they lucked out on the assignment. He'd need to leave a message on his answering machine, too, saying he'd be out of town for a few days.

And Elena. He'd have to give her a call and tell her he wasn't going to make it tonight. If he played his cards right, though, maybe he'd be making it with Sandy. Hell, he might not even have to play his cards right, the way his luck was going. He'd been on a winning streak lately, that was for damn sure.

Sandy was sure it was going to be a stakeout. Maybe not in a van, but somewhere. She hoped it wasn't like the last one in the back of a liquor store, where it was dimly lit, and the air was stale and close. The worst thing about that stakeout was that there hadn't been anything to do for days on end but wait for the robbers to show up. This time she'd pack some books. She knew Chance would bring a deck of cards, but as far as she was concerned, he could play solitaire.

It would be hot and likely dirty. She packed some old gym shorts and T-shirts, and threw in one pair of jeans and a sweatshirt in case of a fluke and there was air-conditioning. She threw in a pair of running shoes to spell the sandals she was wearing.

She wrote out specific instructions for Annie, then went around giving all her houseplants a good soaking. She checked the refrigerator for the expiration date on the milk, decided it might last, and didn't throw it out. She did throw out some wilted lettuce and two tomatoes.

She gathered a dozen books she'd been meaning to read and stuffed them in her satchel. She added toothbrush, toothpaste and a comb, and couldn't think of anything else.

She turned on a lamp so the animals wouldn't be in the dark at night, then turned up the air conditioner a few degrees. So she spoiled them, so what? It made her happy, and it made them happy.

The last thing she did was take Fidel out for a few minutes to let him run around. It was too hot even for Fidel, though, and he usually didn't mind the heat.

It was too hot for anything.

"Don't worry about ironing them, Mom," said Chance in Spanish. "It's probably not going to matter." He was in agreement with Sandy that it was probably going to be a stakeout, but he liked arguing with her.

"You're not walking out of my house with your shirts unironed," said his mother, carrying them over to the ironing board that was always set up in the kitchen.

Chance got some ice water out of the refrigerator and sat down at the table. "I wish you'd let me get you an air conditioner."

"No need," said his mother. "I don't feel the heat."

He felt like saying, *Then why are you sweating so much?* but he knew from experience it wouldn't do any good.

"You call me every day?" she asked him.

"I might not be able to, Mom, but don't worry."

"How do I not worry about my own son?"

Chance glanced over at the small, black-and-white TV, perpetually tuned to Spanish soap operas. He had watched them sometimes as a kid, and he saw they still had the same characters. They didn't even look any older.

"This new partner you like going to be with you?"

"Sandy? Yeah, she's going to be there."

"She's a nice girl?"

"Yes," said Chance, thinking it was unfortunate.

"You should get married, have children."

"Don't start on me, Mom."

"This girl, she's Catholic?"

"I don't think so."

Well, at least that got her off the subject. Married? Children? There had to be more to life than that. His sisters seemed old already, and it had been such a short while ago that they had been blossoming into women.

Chance hated to fold the shirts when they had been ironed so beautifully, but his mother took them from him and did his packing. He tried to slip her some money, but she refused to take it. He finally left some in the kitchen drawer, where he knew she'd find it. Maybe, for once, she'd buy something for herself.

What good was money if he couldn't even help out his mother?

The lieutenant had a map of Dade County spread out on his desk. "This is the route, now pay attention," he was saying as Sandy and Chance leaned over the desk to see where he was pointing. "You're going to be driven here, in a van," he said, pointing to what was a shopping center in south Miami, if Sandy wasn't mistaken. And she was seldom mistaken about the location of malls.

"What'd I tell you," she muttered to Chance. "You owe me five bucks."

"What's that," asked the lieutenant.

"Nothing," said Sandy. "Just a little bet we have."

"She bet me it would be a stakeout," said Chance.

"It's not a stakeout," said the lieutenant.

"I had to pack for a *shopping mall*?" asked Sandy.

The lieutenant straightened and glared at her. "You know, McGee, I thought I picked the right people for this, but you're beginning to make me doubt my judgment."

"Sorry, Lieutenant," she said.

"This is witness protection, highest priority."

Sandy felt a brief surge of adrenaline. "Drugs?"

"Related," said the lieutenant.

Chance let out a low whistle. "Hell, it's the cop case, isn't it?"

When the lieutenant didn't quickly deny it, Sandy gave him a look of chagrin. "It's not, is it?"

The lieutenant sighed. "If you two have no objections, I'd like to complete the route before we get to the briefing."

Sandy could tell Chance minded waiting as much as she did, but neither of them said anything. She only hoped they weren't going to be protecting a bent cop. If there was anything she despised, it was a crooked cop. And a crooked cop who was snitching on his buddies was even worse.

"Okay, here," said the lieutenant, once more pointing to the map. "This parking area is where you'll be let out. Go into the mall, kill a half hour or so, and then you go out the back entrance of Sears and find a light blue '87 Nova, license number 58Z 9R2. The door'll be open, and the keys'll be under the seat. The house key will be on the ring."

"If no one's stolen the car by then," joked Chance.

The lieutenant didn't acknowledge the humor.

"We're going to look pretty weird walking around the mall with luggage," said Sandy.

"No luggage," said the lieutenant. "Your stuff'll be in shopping bags. You'll make the exchange in the van."

"And from there?" asked Chance.

"From there," said the lieutenant, "you'll proceed to Miami Shores. We got you a two-bedroom house where you'll be rendezvousing with the witness."

"He'll be there?" asked Sandy.

"Why do you assume it's a he?" asked Chance.

"Because I have a feeling it's a corrupt cop," said Sandy, "and women aren't corrupt."

"Is that what you think?" Chance asked.

The lieutenant gave them a silencing look. "No, he won't be there. He'll be brought in after dark by the Feds. You'll be a couple who just purchased the house. He'll be your brother-in-law, visiting. Not that you're to answer any of the neighbors' questions or socialize in any way."

"I hope there's a TV," said Chance.

The lieutenant ignored him.

"We're talking about a cop, aren't we?" asked Sandy.

The lieutenant waved them to chairs. "He's our witness," he said. "He's testifying for us."

"In other words, he's made a deal."

The lieutenant gave her a chilly look. "It's called cooperating, McGee."

"If I have a choice, Lieutenant—"

"You don't have a choice. You two are *my* choice."

"Cheer up," Chance told her. "At least that means he doesn't think we're corrupt."

"I don't know," said the lieutenant. "I think the two of you might drive the guy nuts."

Sandy could feel her face forming a scowl. "I'll guard him, but I'm not going to be nice to him."

"Big deal, you're not nice to me, either," said Chance.

"You'll guard him with your lives," said the lieutenant. "And it just might come to that. Just keep in mind, without him the government won't have a case, and if anything happens to him while he's in your protection, you guys won't have a career any longer."

"This is serious stuff, huh?"

The lieutenant nodded. "You got it, McGee. And I shouldn't have to tell either of you that the only one you have any contact with from now on is me. Now get going, the van's around the back."

Chance stood up and grinned down at her. "If you're nice, I'll buy you some ice cream at the mall."

"Ten days with *him*?" Sandy asked the lieutenant. "This isn't an assignment, it's a punishment."

Chance laughed all the way out the door.

"We don't have to really shop," said Chance, following her into Burdine's department store. "This was just a diversion in case someone is following us."

"I didn't know I'd be staying in a two-bedroom house with two men for ten days," said Sandy. "I need something to sleep in and a robe."

"Not for me, you don't. Personally, I always sleep in the nude."

She ignored his remarks. "I wonder if the house has towels. And sheets."

"What do you think, they're putting us in an unfurnished place? If they don't have towels and sheets, we'll send out for them. We're on an expense account, remember?"

"Why don't you go outside and have a cigarette or something? I'll only be a few minutes."

"I don't smoke."

"Could I have a little privacy?"

He grinned. "I think we're supposed to stay together."

"What do you think, Madrigal, I'm going to disappear while buying a robe?"

"Just pretend I'm not here."

"Right." Which meant, damn it, that she was going to have to buy a robe in the women's department, as it would be too embarrassing to admit she bought most of her clothes in preteen. And that meant it was going to cost more, and she already had a perfectly good robe at home. At least she wasn't going to have to sleep in the back of a van in close quarters with Chance. *Sleep in the nude?* He'd better not try that with her.

He followed her off the escalator and grinned at all the lingerie. She left him handling bras in a suggestive way and quickly found a three-quarter length, white terry-cloth robe in a Petite and carried it to the cashier. She'd be damned if she'd look at pajamas with him watching her. She'd sleep in her T-shirt and wear a robe when she had to leave the room.

"Couldn't you get something a little sexier?" complained Chance.

"So the witness will think I'm coming on to him?"

Chance grinned. "No, so that *I* will."

"It's bad enough having to stay in some house with two men, one of whom I don't even know," she said. "Don't make it worse."

"Maybe something black and silky?"

"Is that what your girlfriends wear?"

He grinned. "What makes you think they wear anything?"

Sandy shut up and took out her charge card. The best way to deal with Chance's suggestive remarks was to ignore them. Not that it stopped him, but sometimes it slowed him down. It was too bad that such a good looking guy had to think with what was encased in his Jockey shorts instead of what was in his head. But that was cops—they were all the same. Which was why she was still single, since all she ever met were cops and criminals, maybe the two most macho classes of men on the face of the earth.

Later, sitting at one of the tables in the ice cream store, Chance was being so unusually quiet that she finally had to ask, "What's the problem?"

He looked up from his caramel sundae. "No problem."

"You're being uncommonly quiet."

"Can't I think once in a while?"

"You were thinking? Gee, Chance, I didn't think you ever thought."

"You got a mouth on you, you know that? You know what I'm talking about?"

"I'm learning it from you."

"Oh, you were just a sweet young thing before I was your partner, is that what you're telling me?"

"They called me Miss Sweetness and Light."

"I bet they did."

"So what were you thinking about?"

A slow smile spread across his face. "Ten days alone with you, McGee."

Sandy was sorry she'd asked. "You're not going to be *alone* with me. We're going to have a houseguest."

"You know what I mean." And if she didn't get the drift of his meaning, the look in his eyes gave it away.

"This is work, Madrigal."

"Yeah, they're actually paying us for it. I would've paid *them* for ten days alone with you."

"Will you stop it!"

"I can't help it, you drive me nuts."

"The only thing that drives you nuts is the fact I'm the only woman who won't jump in the sack with you."

His face assumed its sexy look, which consisted of eyelids at half-mast and a jutting lower lip. And, damn it, it *was* sexy.

"Stop that," she said.

"Stop what?" All innocence.

"Stop looking at me that way."

"Sandy, Sandy, you don't know what you're doing to me, you know what I mean?"

"Finish your ice cream, Madrigal, and let's go."

"Can't wait to get me alone, huh?"

"I was thinking maybe we could to to a movie. This mall has six of them."

"The lieutenant didn't say anything about a movie."

"Well, they're not delivering the witness until after dark, and that's hours from now."

"I don't know, I think we better follow directions."

"Since when have you ever followed directions?"

"I haven't had to—you always do."

"We won't see a movie for another ten days."

"Who cares? Maybe there's a VCR in the house."

"It's not the same."

"It's better. You can put your feet up and relax. Make out if you feel like it, you know what I'm talking about?"

She knew. If there was one thing he wasn't, it was subtle.

She was pretty cute. Sitting there eating her ice cream she looked about twelve years old. A nicely developed twelve, but still twelve. When she looked up and you saw the eyes, she didn't look twelve anymore.

He loved teasing her. She was right, though, half her appeal had to do with the fact that so far she had resisted any suggestions on his part that they get together off duty. She claimed it was because they had to work together, but he thought it was partly to do with the idea that he scared her. Every time he came on to her she backed off, her brown eyes getting big and her entire manner becoming defensive. Either she had no experience, or she had been burned badly in the past.

He thought she played up to her youthful looks. The straight brown bangs across her forehead, the shaggy hair down to her shoulders, the absence of any makeup except for a streak of lipstick in the morning that was worn off by ten o'clock, even the way she dressed, all perpetuated the look of a kid. Hell, his sisters had worn more makeup and dressed in a more adult manner when they had been in grade school. Of course, his sisters had been hell on wheels, too, both of them pregnant before they were out of high school, and now he had more nieces and nephews than he could easily count.

Ten days alone with her and maybe he could soften her up. Trying would at least relieve the boredom of ten days of confinement with some bad cop who was making a deal to save his own butt.

"Ready to go?" he asked her.

She licked a trace of ice cream out of the corner of her mouth. He was about to say, *Hey, I would've done that for you,* but he decided to lay off that kind of talk until they were really alone. "Okay," he said, getting up and reaching for the shopping bags. "Let's get this show on the road."

It had happened when he'd been taken down for a shower. One of the prisoners had flashed a knife, and he would've bought it except for a quick move on the part of the guard. Now they were keeping him in solitary. It was for his own protection, but Random was ready to climb the walls.

There were cops who wanted him dead; there were criminals who wanted him dead; and there wasn't much difference between the two. All he wanted was for the trial to be over, and then he'd be out of here. Miami. He could easily live without ever having to see it again.

The reading material in jail consisted primarily of paperback romances in Spanish, with an occasional English language Western thrown in. He'd devoured the Westerns, brushed up on his Spanish with the romances, and now he was down to staring at the walls.

He didn't feel safe, even in solitary. The cops could get to him there without half trying, and if any of the guards were in on it, he was a sitting duck. The word was that he was going to be moved to a safe house, but if that meant in Miami, he questioned how safe it was. Still, anything was better than more time in solitary.

Random had always thought of himself as a loner, but this much of a loner he wasn't.

Chapter 2

Is this a slow car or what? I feel like a real jerk driving around in a baby blue Nova, you know what I'm talking about?" Chance had the air-conditioning on, his arm out the open window, salsa music blasting on the radio, and two fingers on the steering wheel.

"Unlike the macho black Mustang you usually drive," Sandy said, tightening her seat belt and wondering at her chances of survival in a head-on.

"Yeah, right," said Chance.

"I'd be happy to drive," offered Sandy.

"Naw, forget it."

"I happen to be an excellent driver."

"I believe you."

"I have a perfect driving record." True, at least, since high school.

"I'm not surprised," said Chance.

"Then why are you the one who always gets to drive?"

"What do you think, I'm going to be seen being driven around by a girl?"

"Woman," Sandy automatically corrected him, not that it ever did a damn bit of good.

"Whatever. Hey, what do you say we drive over to the ocean and take a look?"

"A look?"

"Yeah, maybe walk along the beach."

"I'm kind of anxious to see the house."

"What for?"

"I don't know," she said. "Aren't you even curious about it?"

"About a *house*? What do I care? What is it, you can't wait to start playing house with me?"

"You're impossible."

"What you see as impossible, everyone else sees as lovable."

"Only a mother could love you, Chance," she said, but she knew it wasn't true. Sandy didn't know why his remarks got to her the way they did. It wasn't that the other cops weren't just as bad when it came to suggestive remarks. She guessed she had been spoiled by her last partner, an older man who had treated her like a daughter. Of course, she used to complain about that, too. In a perfect world she'd be partners with another female cop and neither one of them would have to contend with constant sexual harassment on the job. Actually, she hadn't thought of it as sexual harassment before, but now that she realized that was what it was, she said, "You know, I could get you up on charges, Madrigal."

"What the hell you talking about?"

"Sexual harassment."

He turned his head so fast in her direction he swerved into the next lane.

"Watch where you're going!" she yelled at him.

"Sexual harassment? Are you putting me on?"

"What do you call it, always making remarks to me?"

"You want to know what I call it?"

"Yes, I do."

"Flirting. But I guess that word isn't in your vocabulary."

"The thing about flirting is, it's generally reciprocated."

"I know. I don't know what your problem is."

"And if it's not reciprocated, the one doing the flirting ought to get the message and wise up."

"I get the message—you're playing hard to get."

"I'm not *playing*!"

"I figure ten days alone, I'll soften you up."

"Keep dreaming, Madrigal."

"Sometimes dreams come true."

"You sound like a bad movie."

"How come you talk so tough, McGee? Is it because of your size? Are you compensating or something?"

"Give it a rest, Madrigal."

"I'd really like to know."

"Get off at the next exit and take Biscayne."

"I was going to," said Chance.

"Sure you were."

"What do you think, I don't know my way around? I used to date a lady living in Miami Shores."

"Knowing you, she was probably no lady."

"Is that what you think?"

"I hit the mark, didn't I?"

"For your information, she was a schoolteacher. Yeah, fooled you, didn't I? You didn't figure I'd date schoolteachers."

"I figure you'd date *any*thing."

"Who do you date?"

"I don't feel like discussing it," said Sandy.

"Well, I know you don't date cops, 'cause I've asked around. Everyone says you have an attitude."

"An *attitude*?"

"Yeah, 'cuz you don't date cops."

"That's having an attitude?"

"If you're another cop, it is."

So she didn't date cops? So what? Dating another cop was asking to have your private life discussed by the entire department. Male cops were like jocks when it came to talking about women in the locker room. And the idea of dating her partner was crazy. What happened when they broke up? It would be impossible to still be partners. Okay, so she knew of a few cases where cops married other cops, and she knew about many cases of cops dating other cops. It wasn't for her, and even if it were, it wouldn't be with Chance. Chance just wanted another notch on his belt.

A mile down Biscayne Chance pointed past her out her window. "You see that place over there?"

"With the security guard?"

"Yeah. Somoza used to live there."

Sandy turned around for a better look. "If I had his kind of money, I'd live on the water."

"If I had his money, I'd live in the Bahamas."

"What for?" she asked. She'd been on one disastrous vacation to the Bahamas and failed to see its attraction.

"I like the casinos."

"You gamble?"

Chance turned to look at her. "You kidding me? I *love* to gamble."

"Do you ever win?"

"I make out all right."

He took a left turn into a shopping center, and she was about to ask him where he was going, but then he drove through and out to an access street. A few blocks farther on he took another left, and they were suddenly in an area of houses set back from the road, with large lawns and big trees. It was pretty and peaceful, and she hadn't even known that beyond Biscayne there was such a nice neighborhood.

Chance slowed a little and said, "Look for 326. Never mind, there it is." He pulled into a driveway and parked in front of the attached garage. "Well, sweetheart, we're home," he announced.

Sandy looked out the windshield at a salmon-coloured house with white trim that could use some touching up. The grass needed mowing, but the yard was planted nicely with lots of flowering bushes. "It looks like the lawn needs mowing, dear," she said.

"Forget it," said Chance, getting out of the car.

Sandy got the shopping bags out of the back seat and followed him to the front door. Except for a couple of boys on bicycles, she didn't see any of the neighbors. Even if it hadn't been so hot, she doubted it was the kind of neighborhood where people sat out in their front yards.

Chance unlocked the front door, opened it with a flourish, then stood back to let her enter. "I'd carry you over the threshold, but you'd probably give me a karate chop."

"You better believe it." The first thing she noticed was the heat. "Turn on the air-conditioning—fast," she said to him.

He walked ahead of her and looked around. "I don't think there is any."

"There has to be. Nobody in South Florida lives without air-conditioning."

"Now that's where you're wrong," said Chance. "This place has ceiling fans, and that's all you need. You never get acclimated if you live in air-conditioning."

"You telling me you don't have air-conditioning?"

"My folks don't. Where I live happens to have it."

She watched him as he pulled the cord to the window fan in the living room, then moved farther into the Florida room and did the same thing. Then he opened a few of the windows. Hot, humid air began to circulate.

Sandy thought she was going to die. Ten days without air-conditioning in a heat wave where the temperature hadn't gone below ninety in five weeks was just too much. She went back to the kitchen and looked out the window at the backyard, hoping to see a swimming pool. She didn't. The kitchen, though, was great. It was roomy, with a table and chairs set in front of sliding glass doors that opened onto a patio. She wished her kitchen were that big.

Chance moved into the room and opened the refrigerator. It was empty. "What is this? They're not expecting us to eat?"

"We have time to do some grocery shopping," said Sandy.

"Forget it, we'll order out. We passed some take-out places on Biscayne."

"I'm not spending ten days eating junk food," said Sandy.

"Then you're going to do the cooking."

"I like cooking."

He smiled. "You do?"

She nodded.

"Hey, that doesn't sound so bad. I could use some home cooking."

"As long as you do the cleaning up," she said.

"No problem, the witness can do the cleaning up."

"Wishful thinking," said Sandy.

"Hey, he doesn't help, he doesn't eat."

Sandy moved out of the kitchen and down the hall to the two bedrooms. One was furnished with bunk beds for children. She moved her bags into the room with the queen-size bed and dumped her clothes out on the mattress.

She turned to see Chance standing in the doorway. "This is my room," she said.

"Our room," he corrected her.

"No way."

"Listen, we're going to have to sleep in different shifts anyway. There's no way I'm sleeping in a bunk bed."

She was about to give him an argument, but then decided what he was saying was reasonable. "Is that the only bathroom?'' she asked, pointing to the one connected to the bedroom.

He walked over and looked into the bathroom. ''There's a connecting door to the other bedroom.''

''This is getting a little too cozy for my taste,'' she said.

''There's another one as you first come in,'' he said, ''but it's just a sink and toilet.''

That was okay. At least they wouldn't be lining up at the door. ''Get out of here, I want to change my clothes.''

''Yeah?'' he said, a gleam in his eyes.

''It's a hundred degrees in here, I want to put on some shorts. Do you mind?''

''Not at all. I'll check out the rest of the house.''

Sandy changed into blue gym shorts and a white T-shirt, and pulled her hair on top of her head with an elastic ponytail holder. What she felt like doing was taking a shower, but she'd wait until after they got back from the grocery store.

When she went back to the living room, Chance was spread out on the couch watching a soap opera on TV. ''You actually watch those?'' she asked him.

''I watch anything,'' said Chance. ''I'm a TV junkie.''

''Great,'' said Sandy. ''I hate TV.''

He grinned at her. ''It's fun if you watch it with the right person.''

''I'm going to the supermarket.''

''I'll go with you.''

''Listen, Madrigal, this is getting a little too domestic for me. Why don't you just watch your soaps and when I get back I'll honk so you can help me carry the bags in."

"Bring me back a couple of six-packs."

"We happen to be on duty."

"Twenty-four hours a day?"

"That's right," she said.

"You saying I'm not going to have a beer for ten days?"

Sandy didn't much like the sound of that, either. "I don't think it's a good idea, do you? I guess we could call the lieutenant and ask him."

"Forget it," said Chance. "He'll just say no. But bring me some of those liter bottles of RC Cola. And some nacho chips. Some cheese and crackers, stuff like that."

"Don't you get fat eating that stuff?"

"Do I look fat to you?"

What was she supposed to say, that he had a near perfect body? That was the last thing she'd ever say to him, even if he did look like he worked out every day. Well, she could eat pretty well herself and never hit a hundred pounds on the scale. Which was just as well, Sandy was an even five feet.

"It's so hot, I think I'll just fix us a salad tonight."

"Forget that," said Chance. "Unless you're planning on steaks to go with it."

"I'm not turning the oven on in this heat."

"There's a barbecue on the patio. Pick up some charcoal and lighter fluid and we're in business."

"Is there really?"

"Go look for yourself."

"That's great, I love barbecued food."

He grinned at her. "You mean we finally agree on something? Hey, I'm getting somewhere with you."

Sandy would be almost glad when the witness arrived. At least Chance would have to knock off that kind of talk. With her luck, though, the witness would turn out to be worse.

"You're cleaning up for some crooked cop? I don't believe this."

"I'm cleaning up for me," said Sandy. Whoever had been in the house before them had not been a good housekeeper. The place was neat and looked good at first glance, but there was a layer of dust over everything, and the bathroom was disgusting. She wouldn't even take a shower until the tub was scoured.

"You make me tired just watching you."

"Then quit watching me." She was down on the floor wiping off the baseboards. Her white T-shirt had gotten so filthy she might as well cut it up for dust cloths.

"I think we ought to talk about shifts."

"I'm listening."

"How many hours of sleep do you like to get at night?"

"How many do I like? As many as I can get."

"I'm serious."

"So am I."

"Could you get by on six? With maybe a nap in the afternoon?"

"I guess," said Sandy. "Which six are we talking about?"

"What I figure," said Chance, "is that you could sleep from ten to four and then I'll sleep from four to ten."

"Ten at night? There's no way I could get to sleep that early."

"You'd rather have four to ten?"

"Much rather."

"If he stays up past ten you're going to have to entertain him."

Sandy gave this a little thought. "I'll encourage him to go to bed early, then you can entertain him in the morning."

"He's a cop, right? He probably plays poker. I'll win his money off him in the morning. You mind getting me some more soda?"

Sandy gave him a long, hard look. "I don't believe I heard you say that."

"What's the matter?"

"You asking me to wait on you, Madrigal?"

"As long as you're up."

"I'm not up, I'm on my knees!"

"Sorry," he said, managing to finally get up off the couch. "Can I bring you anything?"

"I'll have a can of iced tea."

"Canned iced tea?"

"I made a pitcher, but it's not cold yet."

When he came back with the drinks she said, "Before you sit down, would you mind helping me move the couch?"

"It's perfect where it is, right across from the TV screen."

"I want to clean behind it anyway, and I thought it would look better in front of the windows."

"I can't see the TV from there."

"So we'll move the TV."

"There'll be a glare on the screen."

"So close the blinds!"

"Okay, okay," he said, and helped her move the couch. Underneath she found thirty-seven cents in change, a ton of crumbs and a lottery ticket. She hoped it hadn't been a winning number.

"That a lottery ticket?" asked Chance.

"Yes."

"You play?"

"No."

He gave her a disbelieving look. "You never play the lottery?"

"No."

"I play it all the time, but so far I've only won five bucks."

"How much have you lost?"

"You can't think of it in those terms. Someday I might hit it big. And you know what I'd do with the money?"

"Move to the Bahamas and gamble it away."

"I'd buy a cigarette boat, and I'd sail it to the Bahamas and then gamble away my money. What would you do if you won?"

"I told you, I don't play."

"But if you did."

"I'd probably buy the cottage I'm renting and put the rest in the bank."

"You have any idea how boring you are, McGee?"

"If I'm so boring, why don't you leave me alone?"

"I keep thinking one of these days you'll change."

* * *

Chance got the barbecue ready, and then, while Sandy was making the salad, he went into the bedroom to use the phone. If she walked in on him, he'd hang up and say he'd just been checking with the lieutenant. What was she going to do, question him? *No way.*

"Put me through to Rivera," he said to the jerk who always answered.

"He's busy."

"Believe me, he's going to want to hear this."

"Hang on a minute."

As soon as Rivera answered Chance said, "You're not going to believe this."

"Try me."

"That special assignment I told you about? It's witness protection in the police corruption trial."

"A cop?"

"You got it."

"Take him out."

"What are you, crazy? I'm here with my partner. If I take him out, I have to take her, too."

"So what's the problem?"

"Right, which leaves me looking guilty as hell. In case you haven't heard, they've got the death penalty in this state."

"Give me your location. I'll have it taken care of."

"If you're going to blow up the house or something, I want to know about it in advance."

"You worried about your hide? Listen, Madrigal, you're more valuable to us alive."

"It can't look like an inside job."

"How's it going to look like an inside job? It's *not* an inside job. How long you going to be there?"

"Ten days."

"And the address?"

Chance rattled it off, ending with, "Look, give me a couple of days first, okay? Otherwise it's going to look bad."

"No problem."

"Can I have some more of that coffee?"

Sandy glared at him. "What did I tell you before?"

"Can't we have a little give-and-take here? I'd be glad to get you some more."

"Fine."

Chance remained seated. "I cooked the steaks, didn't I?"

"Big deal. I fixed the salad and made the chocolate mousse pie."

"And it was delicious. I had three pieces, didn't I?"

"And I set the table, so you're clearing it off."

"I don't see why you didn't buy some paper plates while you were at it."

"I hate eating off paper plates."

He went to the kitchen and got the coffeepot, setting it on the table when he got back. "Listen, I made a phone call before," he said, in case she had heard him and wasn't mentioning it.

"The lieutenant told us—"

"The hell with what he told us. I remembered I hadn't called my mother. If she can't get me on the phone, she'll call the cops and report me missing. I told her not to expect to hear from me for the next ten days.''

"That's nice,'' said Sandy.

"Nice?''

"That you called your mother.''

"You don't know my mother. She'd kill me if I didn't check in.''

"I ought to check on my animals.''

"Go ahead, the phone's working.''

"Annie might not have gotten over there yet.''

"When's it get dark, another hour?''

"About that.''

"I wonder what he's like.''

"He's a cop, isn't he? He's probably just like you.''

Chance grinned. "Then I guess it's going to be your lucky day.''

She barely resisted pouring the coffee over his head. "Why do you think he did it?'' she asked him.

"Money.''

"That's the only reason. Money?''

He shrugged. "What else is there?''

"Would you do it for money?''

"I don't know, Sandy. I'd like to think I wouldn't, but everyone has a price.''

"I don't.''

"Everyone.''

"I don't believe that, or every cop would be corrupt.''

"Look at the countries that produce the drugs. All the cops there *are* corrupt.''

"They're poor countries.''

"You're not interested in money?''

"Not really," said Sandy. "I have everything I want."

"You like animals, right?"

"I love animals."

"With enough money, you could buy your own zoo."

Sandy thought of having her own Bengal tiger and a zebra or two. Maybe some giraffes.

"See? You can be bought," he said.

"I don't need my own zoo. Miami's zoo is great."

"Yeah, but it's not yours."

"Well, I'll tell you something," said Sandy. "Maybe I could be bought. I don't think so, but maybe that's only because I don't want anything that much. But I could never snitch on my friends."

"A bad cop doesn't have any friends."

"Are you telling me you could *snitch*?" She felt incensed enough to kick him.

"Hey, I didn't say that," said Chance, raising his hands in surrender.

"Okay," she said.

"You really have a low opinion of me, don't you?"

"I couldn't be bought, not even for a zoo. And I don't think you could, either."

Chance grinned. "I just like to see you get riled."

"Well, you'll see it again if you don't start cleaning up. Come on, he'll be here in less than an hour."

"I don't believe this, you want the house to look good for some corrupt cop?"

She thought for a moment and realized she did. "You're right," she said, "that's sick behavior, isn't it?"

"Don't sweat it," he said. "My Mom's the exact same way."

* * *

John Random looked out the car window at Biscayne Boulevard. "Who's guarding me?"

Agent Beck turned around in the passenger seat. "A couple of cops named McGee and Madrigal. You might've heard of Madrigal, he was the one rescued the kid from the alligator last year. Made all the papers, and he got some kind of medal for it. He's got a good reputation, kind of a hotshot, but a good man to have on your side."

"And McGee?"

"Unknown quantity."

"There's no such thing as a cop who's an unknown quantity. Come on, what's the scuttlebutt?"

"I don't know anything about McGee other than she and Madrigal are partners and Lieutenant Wainger says you can trust them with your life."

"That's exactly what I'll be doing."

"Wainger's a good man. Other than us and Wainger and the two cops, no one knows the location."

"Maybe I should've stayed in jail for ten days."

"That's the *worst* place you could be. Three of the people you're testifying against were also in that jail. Plus God knows how many on their payroll. Forget the incident with the knife. They did a strip search after that and found plastic explosives."

"If they're going to get me, they're going to get me," said Random, wondering where the plastic explosives had been hidden and having a pretty good idea. The thought made him smile.

"Great, just what we need," said Beck. "That's the kind of attitude that gets people killed. And if you get killed, Random, our case goes down the drain."

"You're wrong, that's the kind of attitude that's going to keep me alive. If I think I'm invincible, they'll get me for sure. Don't worry, Beck—I'm not ready to die.''

Agent Canfield, who was driving, turned left and headed down a dark street. Random couldn't see any sidewalks and very few lights. It was a normal looking middle-class neighborhood, the kind he seldom had any contact with. Most of the houses were set far back from the street and hidden behind shrubbery. He saw the bluish lights of television sets flickering in some of the windows of the houses they passed, and then Canfield was stopping in front of one. This one had a bluish light, too, and he pictured the two cops inside watching some cop series on TV. He wished he had a couple of books with him to read.

"This is it," said Beck. "We'll hand you over to them and be on our way. See you in court in ten days."

They got out of the car, and the two agents escorted him up to the door. He was carrying a bag of essentially dirty clothes, and he hoped the house had a washing machine.

Beck knocked on the door, and it was opened by either a kid or a very small woman. Random hoped they had the wrong house. If by some twist of fate this was McGee, he'd slit his throat.

"Agent Beck," said Beck, showing her his identification.

The woman looked at Canfield, who took out his ID and handed it to her. She studied it, then handed it back, her eyes going to Random.

"I'm McGee," she said to him in a voice that could have chilled a sauna. "Come on in, we've been expecting you."

Chapter 3

Forget it," said Random, turning around and heading back to the car.

The two agents closed in on him.

"I mean it," he said. "Take me back to the jail."

"Don't go by her looks, she's a cop," said Beck, striking a conciliatory note, while Canfield put out a hand to stop him.

Random exploded. "Would you want her protecting *you*?"

"We got a problem out here?" he heard someone say. He turned around and saw a muscular guy standing in the doorway in tight black pants and an open short-sleeved shirt that showed off his pecs and his biceps. Okay, that was more like it, but why weren't there two of *him*?

"Yeah, there's a problem," said Random, cooling

off a little. "I'm not looking to get killed being protected by some midget cop."

The guy gave him a disarming grin. "You must be talking about Sandy. Let me tell you, appearances are deceiving. That one could kill you with her mouth."

The midget pushed her way around the man in the doorway and walked right up to Random, arms folded across her chest, lower lip jutting out. Of course she had to look up at him, which kind of spoiled the effect she was going for with her militant stance. "Listen, buster," she said to him, "the fastest way to get killed is to stand out here and broadcast who you are. I don't like this any more than you do, but if I can stand to protect you, you can damn well stand the protection."

She was right about getting in the house. Already one of the neighbor's porch lights had gone on. He wasn't finished with the midget business yet, not by a long shot.

They all went inside, where Beck and Canfield formally turned him over to them. It was like a scene from some bad cop movie, where the audience knew the witness was as good as dead when they saw the size of one of the cops. The audience probably broke up at that point. There'd be this cute little cop, and you'd know she had to be the love interest, because there was no way she was going to be any good for anything else. Except this wasn't a comedy, this was real life.

"Take good care of him," said Beck. "he's our star witness."

"I'll bet he is," said the midget, and she didn't sound friendly. And an unfriendly guard was no guard at all.

"Not so fast," said Random, as the agents were starting to leave. "I want you to pass on my complaint and get a replacement out here tomorrow. I don't care if it's a female, but I want her regulation size."

He heard a bark of laughter and turned to see the other cop, Madrigal, who seemed to be enjoying the moment hugely. "After that remark, I'd sure hate to be you for the next ten days," Madrigal told him.

"I just want to stay alive for the next ten days."

"We'll pass on your complaint," said Beck, "but don't expect any miracles."

They left before he could ask them what was so miraculous about finding a normal cop. He thought it was miraculous that this one had gotten on the force to begin with. He knew the standards had been lowered, but get serious.

Madrigal was still grinning as he locked the door. "Chance Madrigal," he said, as he held his hand out.

Random paused. "I guess you're going to have to call me John Doe." At least the John would be familiar.

"Well, Johnny, welcome to our happy home."

Johnny? He hadn't been called Johnny since kindergarten. Somehow, though, he didn't mind Madrigal calling him that.

The midget seemed to have disappeared. He looked around the room and saw that the drapes were open and most of the lights were on. "Would you mind closing those?" he said to Madrigal.

"You're right, I should've thought of that," said Chance, going over and pulling them shut. "It's not likely you were followed, is it?"

"It's always possible."

He saw the midget enter the room and stand staring at him. She was looking at him like he was something that had crawled out from under a rock. Not only a big mouth, but also judge and jury, from the look of it.

Chance, still grinning, said, "Johnny, meet Sandy McGee. She's got a mouth on her, but she's cute."

"Stuff it, Madrigal," said the midget.

"See what I mean?" asked Chance. "On the other hand, she's a black belt in karate and wins medals with her marksmanship."

"And I have a brain in my head, unlike some people," she said.

"These females, you got to humor them," said Chance. "They think they're smarter than us just to compensate for their size. They're cute, though, so we let 'em get away with it."

The midget gave him a look that would have turned an ordinary man to stone.

"In this corner," said Chance, pointing to Sandy, "we have lightweight champion Sandy 'The Mouth' McGee, weighing in at eighty-five pounds." He went light on the weight to annoy her. "And in this corner—" pointing to Random "—we have Johnny 'The Witness' Doe, weighing in at, what is it, about one hundred and sixty? Okay, shake hands, go to your corners, and when I whistle, come out fighting!" He let out an ear-shattering whistle, then gave them a wide grin.

"Very funny," said McGee.

"Well, now that you two are acquainted," said Chance, "I think it's my bedtime. See you in six hours, McGee."

Random saw her turn furious eyes on her partner. "You're going to bed *already*?"

Chance looked at his watch. "I should've been in bed twenty minutes ago. Listen, guys need their beauty sleep, too."

"You got anything to drink?" Random asked them.

McGee pointed to a door. "The kitchen's through there."

Obviously they weren't going to furnish room service. Or at least she wasn't. He'd wait until morning to bring up the matter of his dirty laundry. Not that he couldn't do it himself, if she pointed out the washing machine.

Random walked out to the kitchen and turned on the overhead light. Sliding glass doors to the outside and a window over the sink were uncovered. He tried the sliding glass door and found it unlocked. He also tried another door and found it connected to the garage. If this was someone's idea of a safe house, he'd be dead before the week was out. Who was protecting him, a couple of traffic cops?

"Would you get in here, McGee?"

When she didn't rush to do his bidding, he raised his voice. "If I could *please* see you in here for a moment." Okay, so the "please" sounded sarcastic; he couldn't help the way he was feeling.

She appeared in the doorway, a put-upon look on her face. He wondered if she ever smiled.

"I think we have a problem here," he said.

She waited him out.

"The door to the garage isn't locked, the doors to the yard aren't locked, and none of the windows is covered. It looks rather like an open invitation for someone to kill me, wouldn't you agree?"

She obviously didn't, judging by the expression on her face. "We can lock the doors and cover the windows and any interested burglar could still get in. You can open the front door with a credit card."

He leaned back against the kitchen counter. "Why don't you just put a sign outside inviting people in?"

"If someone wants to get you, mister, windows and doors aren't going to stop him. What's going to stop him is me or my partner."

"Somehow that doesn't reassure me."

She walked over to the sliding glass doors, locked them, and then pulled the drapes across. She also locked the door to the garage. Then she reached around him and pulled the blind down over the kitchen window.

She gave him a look that seemed to ask him, *Do you feel safe now?* and then headed out of the kitchen, pausing for a moment in the doorway. "If you'll excuse me, I want to watch the news."

It looked as though it was going to be a long ten days.

The main thing about him was that he looked dangerous. She particularly didn't like his eyes, a shadowy green with a slight slant. She knew that crooked cops came in all styles, but John Doe could be a prototype. Chance seemed to have become friendly with him fast enough. *Johnny*. She'd be damned if she'd call him Johnny. She wouldn't call him anything.

She turned on the TV and sat down on the couch. The lead story was the first of the season's tropical storms, this one heading for the Caribbean. The only time the weather report in Miami got interesting was during hurricane season. The rest of the year they showed the weather around the country, inviting comparisons, no doubt.

She saw him coming into the room, holding a glass of iced tea, and she put her legs up on the couch in case he took it into his head to join her. She ignored him, and he took a seat in the only chair, upholstered but not comfortable. He was wearing worn jeans, faded and fraying, that were low-slung and clung to his narrow hips. His plain white T-shirt was hanging out of his pants and on his feet were dirty white Reeboks.

She hoped he would go to bed pretty soon. It was unnerving having to sit in the same room with him. She wondered how a bent cop felt staying in the same house with a couple of honest ones. He probably couldn't care less.

"What are the sleeping arrangements?" he asked.

She let him wait until the first commercial came on, then she said, "You've got the room with the bunk beds."

He got up and pulled his chair around a little so he had a better view of the TV. She could see dust under the chair and wished she'd thought to move it when she vacuumed. Chance had been complaining about the noise, and she'd done a fast job of it.

He slid down in the chair and stretched his legs out. He wasn't more than an inch or so taller than Chance, maybe five ten, five eleven, but he looked taller, because he had a wiry build. Obviously he did something else with his time other than lift weights like Chance did. Probably something illegal. Seen from the side she saw that his dark brown hair, which she thought had been slicked back, was tied at the back of his neck with a leather thong. It was longer than hers. Not regulation, so he must have been undercover. Which probably meant he'd done a hell of a lot of damage. And now he thought he could make it up by squealing? The man was detestable.

News about the upcoming police corruption trial came on, and she reached for the remote control and pushed the mute button.

"Was that out of deference to me?" he asked, sounding as though he was laughing at her. He spoke in a slow cadence, with the hint of a regional accent she couldn't place.

"It's because it makes me furious to hear it." That ought to shut him up.

When he didn't reply she glanced over to see his reaction and found him giving her a measured look. She scowled and looked back at the TV. It was another commercial, so she turned the sound back on.

The next news story was about a sting operation, and Sandy saw two of the cops she'd gone to the police academy with, both of them working undercover now. Probably not anymore, though, since half of Miami was now seeing them on the news. She'd asked for undercover work once, but Lieutenant Wainger had turned her down. She had accused him of being overprotective of her, but he had just laughed. Maybe after this assignment she'd ask him again.

John Doe had been right. She and Chance should have beefed up the security on the house. Hell, a burglar alarm system wouldn't be out of place. Some safe house, when anyone could walk right in. She figured that if someone came for him, it would be with assault rifles, and she and Chance would probably be taken out with him.

The baseball scores came on, and Sandy turned the set off.

"Do you mind?" he asked.

She turned it back on.

"I take it you don't like baseball?"

"I play on a softball team, but if you mean do I like watching men play it, the answer is no."

"Shortstop, right?"

She ignored him.

When the news was over she turned off the TV and reached for the book she had been reading when he arrived. He might as well learn right now that she watched the news but nothing else. If he liked TV, he could watch soaps with Chance.

He sat quietly for a few minutes while she tried to concentrate on her detective novel. The trouble was, the situation she was in was more interesting than the one in the book.

She finally looked over at him and saw him watching her. There was something about his face—the triangular shape, the high cheekbones, the narrowed eyes and thin, hard mouth—that scared her. She was about to tell him to knock it off when he said, "You got anything else to read?" and she relaxed a little.

She pointed to the books she had brought along, which were piled up on a table. She watched as he got up to take a look.

"*A Brief History of Time*? Are you serious?"

"I keep telling myself I should read it." But she said it grudgingly. She didn't want to have a conversation with him. So he read books? So what? Charles Manson probably read books, too.

She saw him pick it up, read a little; then he turned around and caught her staring at him. "I think I'll hit the sack. Any instructions?"

She gave him a blank look.

"I don't suppose there's an air conditioner in this place."

"No."

"Well, I'm not sleeping with my window closed."

"I saw a window fan out in the garage. You can use it if you want."

He gave her a suspicious look, as though she were setting some kind of trap for him.

She got up, saying, "I'll do it." When she got to the garage, though, he was right behind her, and he was still carrying the book. He took the dusty window fan from her and went back inside. As she was locking the door she said, "You don't trust me, do you?"

"I'm in a position to know that not all cops are honest."

She allowed the corners of her mouth to curve up as she said, "Well, maybe you'll be able to sleep tonight anyway."

His eyes narrowed for a second, and then he turned around and headed down the hall. "Leave your door open," she called out, right before she heard a door being slammed shut.

Not even midnight and the neighborhood was dead quiet. No barking dogs, no traffic, none of the noise she was used to hearing in Coconut Grove, even over the din of her air conditioner. She heard the sound of the shower being turned on and hoped he wasn't the type to leave the bathroom a mess. Who was she kidding? They were all the type. There would probably be a contest between John Doe and Chance to see who could pile up the most wet towels on the bathroom floor. And she'd end up cleaning up after them, because she couldn't stand a mess.

And what the hell was she going to do until four in the morning?

"What? What?" He opened his eyes to see Johnny looking down at him.

"You were asleep."

"Hey," said Chance, "I was only resting my eyes."

"I could hear your snores all the way down the hall."

Chance took his feet off the coffee table and shoved himself up into a more upright position on the couch. He must've forgotten to put the TV on. "What time is it?"

"Twenty after four."

Chance shook his head. "I guess I better do something before going from the bed to the couch. Sorry, next time I'll take a cold shower."

"Maybe you ought to take one now."

"Hey, sit down a minute, Johnny, talk to me. How'd you get along with McGee?"

Johnny sat down on the arm of the couch. "We're not exactly on friendly terms."

"Friendly? Oh, hell, Sandy's never friendly. I had a rough time with her at first until I learned how to handle her. The thing about Sandy is, she's a cop, and she thinks she wants to be treated like a cop, but deep down she wants to be treated like a woman, you know what I mean?"

"I don't think the two are mutually exclusive."

"Take me, for instance. I like to kid her a lot. She acts annoyed, but she really eats it up. She's got this thing for me, but she refuses to admit it."

"Thing?"

"I guess you'd call it a crush. She'll try to act cool 'cause you're around, but you can see it in the way she looks at me."

"I'm more interested in whether she's a good cop."

"Oh, yeah, she's a good cop. I don't know how she is under fire, we haven't run into anything yet. But I get the feeling I could depend on her in an emergency."

"That's reassuring."

"Hey, we're going to take good care of you, Johnny. Wouldn't want anything to happen to the star witness. Those Feds, they're too much sometimes, huh?"

"I'm not too impressed with the security around here," said Johnny.

"Listen, the security is no one knowing we're here. If they know we're here, no amount of security is going to help, short of bullet-proof doors and windows and a nuclear missile on the roof."

"I guess."

"You having trouble sleeping?"

"Not really. The fan in the room helps."

"What fan?"

"There was a window fan in the garage."

Chance tried out his grin on him. "You play poker?"

"I've played."

"How about a game?"

"I'd like to get some sleep."

Chance got to his feet. "Yeah, okay. I'll go get myself some coffee. Listen, sorry about before, it's just that last night I didn't get much sleep." But he was talking to himself, because John Doe had already left the room.

He went out to the kitchen and put on some water to boil. What he would have liked to do was crawl into bed with Sandy. That would be guaranteed to keep him awake all night.

Sandy staggered out to the kitchen at nine. She was entitled to another hour of sleep, but the house next door had children, and they'd been yelling and screaming for the past hour.

She saw clean dishes in the drainer, a pot of coffee on the stove, and out the window was Chance, wearing a minuscule bathing suit, sunbathing in a chaise. John Doe, in jeans and a white T-shirt again, was sitting on the grass in the shade reading a book.

She poured herself a cup of coffee and carried it out to the patio.

"Good morning," she mumbled.

"You look like hell," said Chance. "Didn't you get any sleep?"

"I always look like this in the morning."

"Well, thanks for warning me."

She saw John Doe look up from the book and give her a slight nod.

"What'd you have for breakfast?" she asked.

"Hey, Johnny's some cook. He made omelets and home fries."

Sandy sat down at an umbrella table that was missing its umbrella. The sun already felt full force, and she wondered how Chance could take it. Not that it was much better in the house; she had woken up soaked.

"Maybe if you'd ask him nice, he'd fix you some," said Chance.

Sandy ignored him.

"So what're we going to do all day?" asked Chance, sounding like a little kid on vacation who wanted to be entertained.

"I figured you'd be watching the soaps," said Sandy.

"They're not on until afternoon."

"Or playing poker," she added.

"You feel like playing?" Chance asked her.

"Not first thing in the morning," said Sandy.

"I say we disguise him and take him to the beach. It's a great day for the beach."

"Get serious," said Sandy.

"I *am* serious."

"I'm not even sure we should be outside. Where's your gun?"

Chance glanced at her robe. "Where's yours?"

"We've got to get organized," said Sandy.

John Doe glanced up from his book. "Have you two ever protected anyone before?"

Sandy stood. "Come on, everyone in the house."

"Who appointed you the boss?" asked Chance.

She sighed. "I'm going to call the lieutenant."

"What're you gonna do, tell on me?"

"I'm going to request some instructions and an air conditioner."

"Now you're talking," said Chance, smiling his approval.

The lieutenant didn't sound as though he was smiling. "Damn it, McGee, do I have to spell it out for you?"

"I would appreciate it," she said.

"You stay in the house, you take turns watching the street, and you keep him away from windows."

"Speaking of windows," said Sandy, "we're all dying of the heat."

"The place isn't air-conditioned?"

"No."

"I don't believe it. Ninety-nine degrees and you don't have any air-conditioning?"

"Could we get one?"

"I'll make arrangements. Just be sure you check the guy out before you let him in."

"I'll not only check him out, I'll kiss him."

"Anything else you need?"

"Chance would like a VCR."

"I bet he would. And ten dancing girls, too, right?"

"Thanks, Lieutenant."

"Just keep alert over there, okay?"

"Will do."

*   *   *

They were sitting around the Florida room in the picturesque but uncomfortable bamboo furniture. "I think we ought to make out a schedule," said Sandy.

"What kind of schedule?" asked Chance. Doe didn't even look up from his book. Either he was a devotee of physics or he was faking it.

"We're going to go nuts otherwise," said Sandy. "I think we should have planned times for meals, exercise, recreation and cleaning up."

"Exercise?" asked Chance. "What do we use for weights?"

"There are other forms of exercise."

"Name one."

John Doe looked up from his book as though waiting for her answer.

"Couldn't we do calisthenics?" asked Sandy.

Chance snorted. "Forget it."

"Then *you* think of something."

Chance gave her his sexy look, which wasn't lost on John Doe.

"*You* forget it," said Sandy.

"What did *I* say?" asked Chance, all innocence now. "I was just thinking maybe we could dance. Aerobics, you know what I mean?"

"You and John Doe are free to do all the dancing you want."

She heard John Doe's chuckle as he turned back to his book.

"How about classes on something?" asked Sandy.

"This isn't summer camp," said Chance. "Why don't you just relax or clean the house or something?"

Sandy got up and went to take a cold shower.

* * *

Chance said, "I think it's her time of month."

Random put down the book. "She's right, you know. We're going to get on each other's nerves very soon."

"She's going to get on *my* nerves with all her talk of calisthenics."

"We're getting too relaxed."

"So what do you want to do, play war games around the house? Or maybe hide-and-seek?"

Random thought that if he could combine Madrigal's brawn with McGee's common sense, he might have himself one good guard. "Do you play chess?"

"Chess?"

Random nodded.

"No, I don't play chess. I play poker, I play roulette, I play the horses, and I play around a little."

"Too bad there's not a volleyball net around."

"It's too hot for volleyball."

"Yeah," said Random.

"Like I said, we should go to the beach."

Random went back to reading.

They were all in the living room, where the window air conditioner had been installed. If you sat close enough to it, it helped.

Chance was watching yet another soap, John Doe had a chess set set up and seemed to be playing himself, and Sandy was going nuts. Where were the excitement and challenge she had sought when choosing police work as a career? For pure excitement, checking groceries had to have this beat. She thought of washing the windows, but she didn't feel like leaving the air-conditioned room.

She was watching John Doe when he looked up at her. "You play chess?" he asked.

"No."

"You want to learn?"

"No" was on the tip of her tongue, but then she thought better of it. It beat staring at the walls with the sound of the soaps in the background.

"Yeah, I guess," she said, moving over to the table and chairs they had moved into the living room from the kitchen.

"How about getting me a soda while you're up?" asked Chance.

Sandy was about to tell him to forget it but felt like some iced tea herself. "You want some iced tea?" she asked John Doe.

"If you don't mind."

At least he was more polite than her partner.

Sandy had always thought chess would be just a more complicated kind of checkers, but it was a lot more than that. After Johnny started explaining about the different pieces for the third time, she thought he would lose patience with her and go back to playing himself, but he went on in the same dispassionate tone of voice until she could remember their names and how they all moved.

"You want to try a game?" he asked.

"You think I'm ready?"

"The only way to learn is to play."

She moved a pawn—what else was she going to do?—and he nodded, studying the board as though she actually knew what she was doing. He moved a pawn, and then it was up to her again.

Sandy moved another pawn, and he studied the board for maybe two minutes. She didn't know what his problem was; it wasn't as though she were going to beat him. Why didn't he just move?

He looked up and caught her scowling at him. "It's a matter of strategy," he said.

"Against *me*? I don't even know what I'm doing."

"For all I know you could be a chess hustler."

"Oh, right."

He had her beat in ten minutes, and he could've done it much faster if he hadn't sat around thinking so much.

"Want to try another?" he asked.

"I'm a whiz at checkers."

"I'm sure you are," he said, as though speaking to a bad-tempered child.

"Okay, but could we play a little faster?"

"There's such a thing as speed chess, but I don't think you're ready for it yet."

"Try me," she said.

This time he beat her in a minute and a half.

"Good spaghetti," Random told her.

"Yeah, it isn't bad," said Chance.

"Thanks," said Sandy.

"I use more oregano," said Random.

"It doesn't have any," said Sandy. "I forgot to buy it."

"Are we going to talk cooking?" asked Chance. "Because if we are, I'm going to turn on the tube."

Random was beginning to sense a little hostility from Chance, which had begun when he taught Sandy the rudiments of chess. In an attempt to be politic he said, "Why don't we play some poker after dinner?"

"Now you're talking," said Chance.

"For money?" asked Sandy.

"Of course for money," said her partner. "What do you think, we're going to play for macaroni?"

"I was just asking," she said.

"Well, prepare to lose your fortune," said Chance. "Unless Johnny here is an ace."

"I've played a little poker," said Random. And he loved to play with guys like Chance, who he was sure tried to bluff with every hand.

"I like hearts," said Sandy.

"Right. A real adult game." Chance grinned at Random.

"Personally, I like bridge," said Random.

They both stared at him in alarm.

"I'm quitting," said Sandy. "I want to watch the news."

"You can't quit when you're ahead," said Chance.

"It's past your bedtime anyway."

"Come on, let's have an all-nighter," said Chance. "Anyway, I'm not sleeping in the bedroom when it's air-conditioned out here."

"Well, you're not sleeping out here."

"I think we should all sleep out here," said Random. "It's cooler, and it's safer."

"If you think I'm going to have a slumber party with you guys—"

Chance was already smiling. "Hey, that doesn't sound bad."

Sandy ignored him and turned on the news. The top story was the tropical storm that had developed into Hurricane Andrew. Their interest abated, though, when they heard it was heading for the gulf.

Random said, "Let's move the furniture into the Florida room and move the mattresses in here. We can change it back in the morning—it'll give us something to do."

"It's okay by me," said Chance.

Sandy asked, "How're we going to sleep shifts when we're all out here? Anyway, I don't think we should be all in the same room if something happens."

"Maybe you're right," said Chance, "but we're all in the same room now."

"It's more likely to happen at night," said Sandy.

"You have statistics on that, or is it just women's intuition?" Chance asked, goading her.

"It's common sense," said Sandy. "Something you'd know nothing about. You think they're going to show up here with assault rifles in daylight?"

"Assault rifles?" asked Chance. "Why the hell would they use assault rifles?"

"Why not?"

"It's as good a guess as any," said Random. In fact, it would be his own guess.

"I still say we should play poker all night," said Chance. "You got to give us a chance to get even."

"I'll give you a chance tomorrow," said Sandy.

Random got up. "I'm going to hit the sack," he said. "If you don't mind a bunk bed," he said to Chance, "I've got a window fan in my room. It's not too bad for sleeping.'' He took note of Sandy's look of approval.

"Yeah, okay," said Chance, getting up. "But I think you two are ganging up on me."

Between the two of them, Random was beginning to feel like a peacekeeper.

Chapter 4

Sandy was bored out of her mind. She had already read four of the dozen books she had brought along; there was nothing of interest on TV at two in the morning, even if she liked TV; she had already gotten down on her hands and knees and scrubbed the kitchen floor; and she was wishing she hadn't been so precipitate in breaking up the poker game. Other than winning, it hadn't been that much fun, though. Chance bet on anything and stayed in every hand, and John Doe played such a conservative game that he dropped out almost as soon as the cards were dealt. Her girlfriends in high school had been better poker players.

She was hungry, too. It was eight hours since they'd had dinner, and her stomach was growling. Maybe she should cook up a few meals in advance and freeze them, only then she wouldn't even have the cooking to do for the next few days.

She'd do what she always did when she was bored and hungry, she'd make brownies. She had bought the ingredients; it would use up a little time, and when they were done she could eat them. Not all of them, she'd leave a few for tomorrow, but at least enough to quell her stomach.

The kitchen was hot, and the oven was going to make it hotter. She opened the sliding glass doors, and a slight breeze came in. One thing about Miami, as hot as it got, there was usually a breeze. She could smell the ocean even this far inland, and it made her want to get in the car and head for the beach. Sometimes she and Annie used to run on the beach at night, staying by the water's edge, where the sand was wet and firm, and always ending up with their shoes soaked. She missed Annie. She missed running on the beach. She missed the freedom of coming and going when she wanted. She hated the waiting, the constant waiting for something to happen and all the while hoping nothing would. She wondered if that would change at some point and she'd start wishing something *would* happen just to break up the monotony of always waiting.

She took out the ingredients and set them on the counter, then found a wooden salad bowl she could use for mixing. Maybe she should have been a chef, or a baker. She got more enjoyment out of cooking than she did out of police work. She thought it was probably her friends' fault, which came of having two best friends who were bent on having exciting careers. How could she tell Bolivia, who wanted to be a foreign correspondent, and Annie, who wanted to be a lawyer, that all she really wanted to do was get married and have a house and some children? So now Annie was a lawyer, but she was also married; and Bolivia was a foreign correspondent, but she was in love with Tooley; and all Sandy had was a partner who was the Don Juan of the police department and a job guarding a crooked cop. She ought to start answering personal ads again; maybe this time she'd get lucky.

She slid the baking pan into the oven and went out to the patio to get some fresh air and cool off.

Random couldn't sleep. Maybe it was Madrigal's snoring; maybe it was because every car passing in the street, every dog barking, every jet passing overhead, raised his level of alertness; maybe it was the fact that he felt as though he was being guarded by two rank amateurs, and he had a feeling he'd be better off climbing out the window and hiding himself until the trial. They probably wouldn't even notice he was gone. Plus, there was also the nagging suspicion at the back of his mind that either one of them could be corrupt and tied in to the trial, in which case he didn't have a prayer.

What he hated was the lack of control. He wanted to be in charge. He would've liked to pick out the safe house, choose his two guards and call the shots.

He had nothing personal against Madrigal and McGee. He'd read about Madrigal in the newspaper, heard about his feats of heroism from other cops. He was much admired in the force, and he supposed he should be thankful someone like that was guarding him. On the other hand, he had also heard Madrigal had been regularly transferred around the department by his supervisors because he didn't always follow orders and they considered him hard to handle. Still, the guy was likable, even if he wasn't mentally stimulating.

He raised his head and sniffed. He could swear he smelled chocolate.

McGee he couldn't get a handle on. He didn't appreciate her size, that was a given, but she took the job more seriously than Madrigal, and she had shown a quick intelligence when he was teaching her chess. He had also loved the way she had whipped Madrigal at poker. Of course, she had whipped him, too, but not nearly as badly. He'd never gone for short women, and he usually preferred them more sophisticated, but Sandy was appealing. He realized, though, that ninety percent of that appeal probably had to do with the fact that she was the only woman in the house. And maybe it had something to do with competitiveness, too. Chance was after her, and he thought she was too good for Chance.

He did smell chocolate; he was sure of it. And why would he be smelling chocolate in the middle of the night? Looking at it logically, McGee had to be cooking something. Being a chocolate buff, he climbed down from the top bunk quietly, put on his jeans and sneaked out to the kitchen.

She *was* baking something, because the kitchen was hot, and the smell was stronger here. He saw that the sliding glass door was open and was ready to curse at the lack of security when he saw that she was sitting outside. He stepped softly onto the patio.

"What are you doing up?" she asked him.

"I couldn't sleep, and I smelled chocolate."

"I'm making brownies."

He felt his mouth begin to water. He decided to make an effort not to rile her so that maybe she'd offer him some.

"Is it the heat?" she asked him.

"It's not that bad in there tonight."

"Chance's snoring?"

"Partly, I guess."

"If you're not tired, feel free to use the living room."

"Thanks."

She gave him a measuring look. "Are you nervous?"

"Nervous? Hell, I'm downright scared."

"Are you that much of a threat?"

"I'm sorry, I can't discuss the case." Yeah, he was a threat—to the cops and the drug kingpins. And a bigger danger to McGee and Madrigal than they seemed to realize. The people he was testifying against had found and killed witnesses—and those protecting them—in more difficult-to-find locations than this.

Sandy got up. "The brownies should be ready." When he started to follow her she said, "You can stay where you are. They have to cool off for ten minutes."

"How can you wait?" he asked.

"Well, a couple minutes, anyway."

He watched her through the glass door. He had noticed before that she looked serious and efficient when she was cooking. He wished she looked as serious and efficient the rest of the time. She was wearing her gun, though, stuck into the waistband of her shorts. It couldn't be comfortable, and it looked ridiculous, but at least she wore it, which was more than he could say for Chance most of the time. He'd feel a hell of a lot more secure if they'd let him have a gun. He'd asked but had been refused.

She came out with a plate stacked with brownies and some paper napkins. "You want some coffee to go with it?" she asked.

"No thanks."

"The chocolate has just as much caffeine."

"It's too hot for coffee."

"Iced tea?"

"Let me get it," he said, going into the kitchen and pouring them each a glass. He saw that she had already started in on a brownie when he got back outside, so he didn't hesitate to reach for one. The first bite was hot, but delicious. His mom had made brownies a lot when he was a kid, the tempting aroma permeating their Indiana home. He couldn't remember whether his mom's were as good as these.

"Can I ask you a personal question?" he asked her.

"You can try," she said.

"Why'd you become a cop?"

She gave him a curious look. "I was asking myself the same thing tonight."

"And did you come to any conclusion?"

She shrugged. "I didn't like college, and I wanted a career. And Miami had so much crime, I thought I'd be doing something worthwhile."

"It still does."

She gave him a look that said he was partly responsible for that, and he thought it time to change the subject. "Madrigal seems like a good guy," he said.

Silence.

"I'd heard about him."

"Chance has quite a reputation," said Sandy, her tone noncommittal.

"He seems sweet on you."

She made a low sound that could have been a laugh. "Sweet? Well, that's a nice way to put it, anyway."

Random chuckled. "Okay, so he seems to have the hots for you."

"He's that way with all the women."

"I don't know, the way he watches you, the way he got annoyed when I was teaching you chess."

"Could we change the subject?"

Random reached for the last brownie and then withdrew his hand.

"Go on," she said, "there's more in the kitchen."

"They're really excellent."

"Thanks."

His mouth was half-full of brownie when she asked, "What made *you* become a cop?" and he choked for a minute.

"You okay?"

"Yeah," he said, swallowing some of the iced tea.

"Don't answer if you don't feel like it."

He was still trying to think up a good answer when he heard, "What is this, a party?" and turned around to see Chance coming out the door, barefoot and wearing only a pair of Jockey shorts. He would've figured Chance for the type to wear briefs, particularly after the bathing suit he had sported.

"There's brownies in the kit—" Sandy started to say, and then an explosion ripped apart the front of the house, the force blowing out the glass in the door and throwing Chance forward.

"What the hell?" said Chance, but Random was already diving for the grass, and Sandy was running for the back fence.

Random saw that a piece of the glass must have hit Chance, because he was bleeding from the leg. He was about to mention it when he saw that his own arm was bleeding. He'd take a little blood compared to being blown apart. And that was what would have happened if he had still been in bed. The side of the house where the bedrooms had been was gone.

"Come on, we've got to get out of here," she called back to them, already scaling the chain link fence.

Random looked at Chance, who seemed to be dazed. "You okay?" he asked.

Chance shook his head a little and then said, "Yeah, I think."

"There might be another," yelled Sandy, already over the fence and into the neighbor's yard. Lights were going on in all the houses around them.

"Let's go," said Random, running to the back fence and hearing Chance behind him. He looked back once and saw the house in flames. The bomb would've done the job if he and Chance had still been in the bedroom. Only Sandy would have been okay, and only because of her brownies. And having been taught to be suspicious, he had to consider that fact.

They were around the house and halfway down the block before they heard the first sirens in the distance. People were starting to come out of their houses on this block, too, and Sandy said sotto voce to

Chance, "Get ahead of us and pretend you're jogging."

"Get serious," said Chance.

"You look suspicious out here in your underwear."

"I'd look more suspicious jogging barefoot."

"I think you should do what she says," said Random, and with a disbelieving shake of his head, Chance moved ahead of them and started to jog.

"Where're we headed?" asked Random.

"The nearest shopping center," said Sandy. "When we get to the corner, I'm going to start to run. Try to keep up."

"I'll keep up," he assured her.

She looked down at his bare feet. He realized then that she was the only one wearing shoes. He further realized, when they reached the corner, that he might have trouble keeping up with her even with shoes. For someone with such short legs, she sure had speed. And her legs, which had looked like a kid's before, now looked muscular and strong.

She passed Chance, who was still jogging, and said, "Speed it up, we've got to get out of here."

They were still running when they reached the shopping center. It was dark, and everything was closed. Traffic was still moderate on Biscayne, and a couple of cop cars raced by with their sirens going.

"What the hell did we run here for?" asked Chance. Random had been wondering the same thing.

"We've got to find a pay phone," said Sandy.

"Wait'll the lieutenant hears this," said Chance.

She said, "We're not calling the lieutenant, we're calling a taxi."

"I don't know—" began Chance.

"I do," said Sandy. "We're going to spend the rest of the night in a place no one knows about but us. We'll call the lieutenant in the morning." She gave them each a close look. "You're both bleeding."

Despite the situation they were in, Chance managed to leer at her and say, "Maybe you ought to rip up your shirt for bandages."

"You wish," said Sandy, already walking down the length of the shopping center and looking for a phone. They followed her, but they didn't find one.

Chance said, "Why don't we just knock on someone's door, tell them we're cops and ask to use their phone?"

Sandy gave him a withering look. "You think they'd believe us? I don't know about you, but my ID went up with the house."

Chance looked down at his undershorts with a rueful grin and said, "I guess you're right. But we can't walk down Biscayne looking like this, either."

"Can either of you hot-wire a car?" asked Sandy, her glance going to the lone Honda that was parked in front of the florist shop.

"Yeah, I can wire it," said Chance.

Two minutes later they were on the road.

Sandy overruled Chance for once and got to drive. She kept within the speed limit, but made good time to Coconut Grove. The men were silent during the drive, and she wondered if they were in shock. She wondered if she were in shock, but she didn't think so. Chance, though, was bleeding badly from the leg. "You okay?" she asked him.

"Yeah," he said, but he didn't sound like his usual self.

"What about you?" she asked, looking into the rearview mirror at John Doe in the back seat. "I'm okay," she heard, but his face looked stunned.

"Maybe we ought to go by a hospital," she threw out, although she had no intention of going to one. Not tonight. Tonight she wanted to go somewhere safe, and that wouldn't be a hospital.

"No," said Chance.

"That's the first place they'll look when they find out they didn't get me," said John Doe.

She turned on the car radio and tried to find a station with news. All she got was music and a talk show, and she turned it back off.

She parked the car in front of a restaurant down the street from where she lived and turned off the engine.

"What the hell are we doing here?" asked Chance.

"Dumping the car," said Sandy.

"In *Coconut Grove*?"

"I live in Coconut Grove," said Sandy, getting out and pushing the seat up so that John Doe could get out. She felt like dumping Chance, with all his questions, along with the car.

"I didn't know you lived in the Grove," said Chance.

"There's a lot you don't know about me."

"I come down here a lot," he said, and she knew he was referring to the clubs and the nightlife. Well, tonight "nightlife" had acquired a different meaning for them: it meant bombs going off when you were supposed to be in bed sleeping. It meant running and hiding and bleeding from the leg and wondering how you'd been so lucky.

She saw that her neighbors' houses were dark and hoped Fidel wouldn't start barking at their arrival. Her house was dark, too. Annie must have turned off the light she had left on for the animals. She lifted the potted plant on the front porch and found her extra key, then let them quietly into the cottage.

As soon as she switched the light on, Fidel came bounding out of her bedroom. He made a leap for her arms and she caught him, allowing him to shower her face with kisses, which would take the place of his barking. She didn't see Jackson, who was probably mad at her for deserting him.

"Hey, this is cute," said Chance, looking around. "Cozy. It reminds me of my grandmother's place."

"Did you do the needlepoint?" asked John Doe.

She gave him an exasperated look. What was he, an authority on *every*thing?

"Out in the kitchen, both of you," she said. "I want to take a look at those cuts."

She set Fidel down on the floor, and he started to dance around in circles.

"Cute dog," said Chance.

"His name is Fidel," she said, leading the way into the kitchen. She wondered where Jackson was hiding. He had probably heard strange voices and wouldn't come out.

She sat the two men down at the table and then got hydrogen peroxide and antibiotic ointment for their cuts. John Doe's wasn't deep and was already starting to close, but Chance looked as though he could use stitches.

"Maybe you *should* go to a hospital," she told him.

"Forget it."

"In this climate, it's never going to heal," she said.

"Quit acting like my mother," said Chance. "Just wrap something around it, it'll be all right."

Sandy knew what was needed, and the hell with being on duty. She went to the refrigerator and took out three cold beers.

"That's more like it," said Chance, and even John Doe looked more cheerful.

She took a quick swallow of hers and then went to look for something to use as a bandage. She finally got a clean pillowcase and cut it in strips. If that cut didn't look better by morning, she was going to tell the lieutenant that Chance required hospitalization. Maybe her luck would change and he'd pull them off the job, or at least replace Chance.

"I still think we ought to call the lieutenant," said Chance. "For all he knows, we were all blown up in the house."

"They won't find any bodies," she said, "and he'll know we got away. Anyway, he'd probably send us to a motel for the night, and I'd rather be at home. In case you hadn't noticed, the two of you could use some clothes."

"If you think I'm dressing in your clothes—" Chance began.

She cut him off. "Just shut up and drink your beer." She opened the cupboard and took out a can of cashews, putting it down on the table before going into the bedroom. She slept in extra large men's T-shirts, and she didn't see how they could object to those.

She came back and handed one to each of them. They both put them on, Chance without a murmur, for which she was thankful.

Then she joined them at the table, and shock suddenly set in. "We should be dead, you know," she said, and was ashamed when she heard the quiver in her voice.

Chance looked a little shaken, too. "If I hadn't woken up at just that moment..."

"It was miraculous," said John Doe. "If Sandy hadn't been making brownies—"

"And gone outside to cool off," she added.

"And if I hadn't smelled the chocolate and gone out to investigate—"

"I don't even know what woke me," said Chance.

"At least they didn't get the brownies," said Sandy. "If the bomb had gone off *before* the brownies had been done, I'd *really* be mad."

"They were damn good brownies," said John Doe.

"I didn't even get any," groused Chance, and he sounded more like his old self.

"A bomb," said Sandy. "I wasn't expecting a bomb."

"What were you expecting?" asked John Doe.

"Men in black with assault rifles. You know, like a SWAT team made up of criminals."

"There's nothing we're going to be able to do against bombs," said John Doe. "Not if they know where we are."

"Someone had to tell them," said Sandy. "And the only ones who knew were cops and Feds."

"I don't think it's the Feds," said John Doe. "It's their case. It's got to be one of the cops. How many people knew where we were?"

"I don't know," said Sandy, "but that's going to be the first thing I ask Lieutenant Wainger."

"Half the department was probably in on it," said Chance.

Sandy shook her head. "That's not what the lieutenant told us."

"You know how it is," Chance said to her. "How many times have you known about something that was top secret?"

"Too many," said Sandy.

"Got another of these?" asked Chance, holding up his empty beer can.

"In the refrigerator," said Sandy. "You can get us all one."

"From brownies to beer in less than an hour," said John Doe, lightening the mood a little.

Chance said, "You're missing your sleep, Sandy. Feel free to go to bed. We'll keep watch."

"Sleep? You think I can sleep after that?"

"I think you better try," he said. "You're not going to be much use to us with no sleep."

John Doe glanced up at her. "You did good tonight. You were the only one doing any thinking on your feet."

"That's because she was the only one wearing shoes," said Chance and they all managed to laugh.

"I'm the only one with a gun, too."

"I mean it," said John Doe. "I'm sorry about the 'midget' remark. It's thanks to you we got out of there so quickly."

Jackson stalked slowly into the kitchen, having aroused himself from wherever he had been hiding. "Hey, Jackson," said Sandy. "Come over here so I can give you a hug."

"Look at the size of him," said Chance. "He looks like a black panther." He reached out his hand to the cat and got an instant slash across the back of it.

"That'll teach you to mess with my cat," said Sandy.

Now blood was pouring out of his hand. Sandy handed Chance a paper towel and said, "What are you, a bleeder?"

That started John Doe laughing, and pretty soon they had all joined in.

"You laugh, Johnny," said Chance, "but wait until she starts in on you."

Sandy saw him pausing to jump and was just about to warn John Doe, when Jackson leaped onto his lap and began purring. He seemed to be familiar with cats, because he started scratching Jackson behind the ears. She only hoped a flea wouldn't jump out and embarrass her. Jackson managed to lose every flea collar she bought for him in a matter of minutes.

"Maybe we ought to eat something with this beer," said Sandy.

John Doe gave her a disbelieving look.

"Okay," she said, "so we consumed a dozen brownies. Chance hasn't eaten."

"Got anything for a sandwich around?" asked Chance.

"How about a ham and egg sandwich?"

"Sounds good."

"What about you?" she asked, and when he didn't look up from the cat, she added, "Johnny."

He smiled at her. "I guess I could eat one, too," he said.

She guessed she could, too. There was something about danger that always left her feeling hungry.

"She's sleeping," said Chance, coming back into the kitchen.

"Good."

"She's got more guts than I do. I don't think I could sleep."

"She probably feels safer sleeping in her own bed," said Johnny. "Nice house she has here."

"Too much stuff around," said Chance.

"She's made it into a home."

"She has a well-stocked kitchen, I'll grant you that. And there's a VCR in the living room, and some movies, if you feel like watching."

Johnny shook his head. "I wouldn't mind some more sleep, if it's okay with you. I couldn't sleep earlier."

"There's only one bedroom."

"I don't mind sleeping with the television on. That chair in there looks comfortable."

"Take the couch," said Chance. He'd be better off sitting up anyway. Keep him alert. Not that he thought he was in any danger of falling asleep, not after what Rivera had pulled.

He wondered if Rivera thought they'd bought it in the explosion, or whether he'd already gotten the word. If he'd heard, he must be wondering what Chance was thinking about now. Like, obviously he was expendable. In fact, Rivera might just be wondering if maybe *he* was going to make a deal and testify along with Johnny. Serve him right if he did, damn it.

Chance didn't know what to do now. Sure, he could try to make a deal, but he had thought he had a pretty thing going, and instead his name would be in all the papers, and his mother would probably die of a stroke. If there was one thing she hated it was drugs, especially since his younger brother had died of an overdose. Who was to say the department would even make a deal with him? They might just lock him in the slammer and throw away the key. And cops were never safe in prison. He didn't think he could take prison, anyway. Even something the size of Sandy's house was giving him claustrophobia, all the stuff around crowding him in.

The problem was, the alternative didn't look much better. What was he supposed to do, call Rivera again when he knew their new whereabouts? And have the bomb go off successfully the next time?

More valuable to them alive? Sure, and he'd believed it. Like Rivera didn't ever lie.

What's more, he didn't want Sandy blown up, either. It was one thing setting up a bad cop who was turning state's evidence and quite another to get his partner blown up. Plus he liked her.

He would call Rivera in the morning. He couldn't wait to hear what the man had to say for himself. And it had better be damn good, or maybe he'd just blow the state and start over somewhere else. He knew his way around; he'd do okay.

But he was beginning to wonder if the money had been worth it.

She'd called him *Johnny*. She'd called him Johnny, and she had brought him to her own house and taken care of his wound. If she wanted him dead, would she be doing all that?

She wasn't living above her means, not in this cottage. She didn't wear fancy clothes or jewelry. She didn't have a habit; he could spot someone with a habit straight off. If she were involved, he'd bet it had to do with love. He thought she was the type who might do something like that for love. A safer bet, though, was that she wasn't involved at all.

Chance was a question mark. Yeah, he could be on the take, but if he was involved, why had he almost bought it? A cop, placed like that, would be too valuable to blow up.

It had to be a leak in the department. It had to be, because if he started to think in terms of a leak at the federal level, then he was as good as dead. If there was a leak there, none of them stood a chance.

He liked her house. It was comfortable. It was like being a kid again back home. He'd had a dog when he was a kid, and his mom had always had cats. He'd never had a pet since, and he found he liked having a warm cat in his lap who purred when he touched him. He liked the comfortable overstuffed furniture, too, and the soft pillow covered with needlepoint, and the rag rug on the floor and the plants all over the place. There was a fireplace, and he bet she used it on the few nights when it got cold enough in Miami. He could picture her sitting in front of it, the dog by her feet, a cup of hot chocolate in her hand, probably a plate of brownies on the table. She wouldn't be trying to look like a cop then, and she'd be wearing something soft, maybe a pink wool robe, with furry slippers on her feet.

Hell, he was getting maudlin. He was in jeopardy—*they* were in jeopardy—and this was no time to start to get sentimental over what he had missed in life. He'd made his choices, and this was the result. Now he had to live with it. And after the ten days were up, he'd never see Sandy again.

He shifted in the chair, and Jackson dug his claws into his leg. He put his hand on the cat's head, and Jackson's claws retracted and he started to purr. The dog wasn't around; he must be sleeping with Sandy.

He opened his eyes enough to see Chance on the couch watching an old movie with the sound turned down low. Sandy had left him her gun, and it was on the coffee table within reach.

If he waited long enough, Chance would fall asleep and he could take the gun and let himself out of the cottage and be miles away before they missed him. They'd be safe that way, and he could manage to hide until the trial. Everyone would be better off if he just disappeared.

The beer had relaxed him, though, and he felt stuffed with food, and it was just too much of an effort. And he felt peaceful here, more at home than he could remember feeling in years. Maybe he should go, but he found he wanted to stay.

Chapter 5

Sandy woke up in her own bed and forgot for a minute that she was still on special assignment. She enjoyed the patterns the sun made coming through the white shutters that covered the window. There was something about sunlight on white that pleased her, that captured her attention and made her smile. A crystal hanging in the window caught a rainbow and sent it flying over the walls of the room. Her eyes followed it to her dresser top and her collection of china cats. One in particular, a fat black-and-white cat with bright blue eyes, always made her happy. Bolivia had bought it for her and brought it over wrapped in layers of newspaper and had sat watching Sandy to see her expression the exact moment she caught sight of the cat. She liked the others, too, but the black and white was her favorite.

She was just wondering if it was time to get up—she couldn't remember hearing the alarm—and then Jackson stirred beside her, and she flashed on the scratch he had given Chance and wondered how she could have forgotten how she'd gotten here. Was it wrong to be able to forget for a while? Was it wishful thinking?

She stretched, liking the feel of clean cotton against her body. It felt good to be home and sleeping in her own bed with the flowered sheets, even if it couldn't last.

She got up and peeked out to the living room. Johnny was asleep on the couch, and Chance was watching a game show. Chance looked so normal, Johnny so innocent, did they really have to go back, or could they stay here forever, safe within the walls of her cottage? If she had a wish she would turn back time, go back to before any of it began and start anew. This time Johnny would be a good cop. This time ... She wondered when she had become so fanciful. Something had changed, though; something had been taken out of her when the bomb exploded. And in its stead was a small light place hidden inside of her, and it was slowly, slowly, growing.

She closed her door softly and went back to bed, reaching for the pink phone on her bedside table. She dialed Annie's number at the office.

"Larkin," answered Annie.

"It's me."

"Sandy? Are you back?"

"Only temporarily. I wanted you to know you could take the day off."

"What's happening?"

"Confidential?"

"Of course."

Sandy told her the whole story. After all, if she couldn't trust an officer of the court and her best friend, who could she trust? It wasn't Annie who had given away their location.

"I don't like the sound of this, Sandy," Annie said when she was finished.

"You think *I* do?"

"You guys want to come stay at our place? We can put you up."

"I'd love to, but I'm afraid it's up to the lieutenant."

"It was up to him the first time."

"It wasn't Lieutenant Wainger, Annie."

"And it wasn't you . . ."

"Several people had to know about the location in order to set up the house for us. And for all I know, we were followed."

"I hate it," said Annie. "I hate it that you're in danger and I can't do anything about it."

"The worst happened, and it wasn't so bad."

"The *worst*? That wasn't the worst. If you'd been killed in the bombing, that would be the worst. It's bad enough with Bolivia in Beirut, now I have to worry about you, as well."

"The lieutenant won't put us in danger again. He's a good man, Annie."

"That's what they always say."

"Well, sometimes you have to trust someone."

"I know. I'm just fussing. Don't pay any attention to me. It's my maternal instincts."

"Since when do you have maternal instincts, Annie?"

"I don't know. It's strange, isn't it? I guess since I got married. Suddenly I've realized that everyone's mortal, and I worry about things. I yell at Jack if he doesn't fasten his seat belt in the car, I don't drive as fast anymore, I call my mother almost every day. To tell you the truth, I hope this is just a phase I'm going through, because I really don't like it."

"I've always been like that."

"Well, you, yes, you were always like that. You were born like that. I guess it didn't hit me until I fell in love. So how's it going with Chance?"

"He can be a real pain."

"What's the other one like?"

"Well, he looked kind of dangerous at first, but he's not so bad. Sometimes I find myself forgetting he's a bent cop."

"Maybe he had a good reason."

"Like medical care for his poor, dying mother? Forget it, there *is* no good reason."

"Maybe, but pure greed's the worst."

"They're all equally bad."

"If I know you, being a snitch is the worst of all."

"I always did hate a snitch."

"Is there anything I can do for you?"

"Yeah, you can bring disguises over for all of us."

"That's not such a bad idea, you know."

"I've been thinking about it."

"Except there's no way you can disguise your height, and if they're looking for a—"

Sandy exploded. "Don't you dare say *midget*!"

"I wasn't going to say *midget*. Why would I say a thing like that?"

"That's what John Doe said when he first saw me."

Annie laughed. "That was his first mistake, right?"

"Right."

"You've got me really worried about you, Sandy. I think I'll come over."

"Don't do it, Annie. I'd get in trouble for even calling you. Look, I'll try to keep in touch."

"I'd like to get a look at this dangerous guy."

"I knew it!"

"Just curiosity. And I *am* worried."

"Don't worry, I'll be so careful from now on no one will be able to get to us."

"And you'll call?"

"I'll try."

Chance shook him awake, and the first thing he could smell was pancakes. No one had made pancakes for him since he was a kid. If she made pancakes as good as her brownies, maybe he'd marry her.

"Everything okay?" he asked Chance.

"Yeah. Breakfast's about ready."

Random sat up on the couch. Sometime during the night he must have moved from the chair. It was overstuffed and comfortable, but his back was killing him. "What time is it?"

"Almost noon."

"Anyone called the lieutenant yet?"

Chance shook his head. "Sandy's going to do it after breakfast."

The first thing she said to him when he walked into the kitchen was, "I think we ought to shave your head."

"Are you talking to me?" he asked.

"I've been thinking in terms of disguises. You're pretty recognizable with that ponytail."

"She just doesn't like long hair," said Chance.

"It's not long hair I don't like, it's bombs."

Random said, "They knew the location. They weren't zeroing in on a ponytail."

"I'd still feel better if we were disguised," said Sandy.

Chance sat down at the table and grinned at both of them. "How about this? I'll disguise myself as the father, Johnny—with his long hair—can disguise himself as the mother, and you can disguise yourself as our ten-year-old son."

Random made the mistake of laughing and got a furious look from Sandy.

Chance shrugged. "What do you want? I'm too muscular to be the mother."

"Women have muscles," Sandy informed him.

"Not like mine," said Chance, flexing a few of them. "Not even with steroids."

"Maybe that's not a bad idea," said Sandy.

"Forget it," said Random.

"What are you, too macho to dress like a woman?" asked Chance, a big grin spread all over his face.

"If I can dress like a little boy—" said Sandy.

"You already dress like a little boy," Random informed her, taking in her shorts and striped T-shirt with a glance.

"I can see you don't want any pancakes," she said.

Random shook his head in amusement. "Okay, just for breakfast I'll be the mother."

Sandy placed stacks of pancakes on their plates, with side dishes of sausages. He hadn't eaten so well in years. He also appreciated the cheerful yellow tablecloth and yellow-and-white-checked cotton napkins. She had even set a pitcher of flowers on the table, and they looked so fresh she must have just picked them. He was beginning to feel at home, and that wasn't something he should be feeling.

"The lieutenant's got to be having a heart attack by this time," said Chance, the food in his mouth making him slur his words.

"Don't talk with your mouth full," said Random in a falsetto, which cracked Chance up to where he was choking on his food.

"I don't care if he's having a heart attack," said Sandy. "Someone down there had to have given away our location. Other than Wainger, I don't think I trust anyone."

"You trust him, too?" Random asked Chance.

Chance nodded. "Yeah. The lieutenant's as straight as they come."

"People probably said that about me," said Random, and was sorry as soon as the words were out, because the air suddenly became dead serious. Then Jackson leaped up on the table and broke the mood.

"You let the cat eat on the table?" asked Chance, but Sandy was already picking up the cat and dropping him to the floor. It wasn't a punishment because she followed it with a sausage.

"I've been thinking," said Random.

They both looked at him.

"I might be better off alone. You two would definitely be better off."

"I agree with you," said Chance, "only I don't think the lieutenant will. He just might not trust you to show up in court."

"Why wouldn't I show up? They're dropping the charges against me in return for my testimony."

"Still, you might be thinking you'll be just as easy a target after the trial, and the police won't be protecting you then."

Sandy shook her head. "He's probably going to be in the witness protection program."

"They give that to crooked cops?" asked Chance.

"The Feds do," said Sandy, sounding disapproving.

Random found he had suddenly lost his appetite. He got up from the table and looked out the window. She had a pretty yard, overgrown and tropical. He spied a hammock beneath a tree and a huge doghouse that probably went unused.

"I say we walk into Coconut Grove and see a movie this afternoon," said Chance. "They're not likely to bomb a movie theater."

"You had your chance at the mall," Sandy told him.

"You mean that's it? I only get one chance?"

"That's it," said Sandy. "You'll never get to see another movie again."

Chance said, "Let's drive down to the Keys. No one would think of looking for us down there."

"I still think we should disguise ourselves. Then we could go wherever we wanted."

"Anyway, I wouldn't mind some more of these," said Chance. "Good pancakes, Sandy."

Random was still standing at the window when he heard a phone being dialed. He turned around and saw Sandy using the wall phone.

What he ought to do was bolt out the door. Chance didn't have a gun, and Sandy's wasn't in evidence. He was about to take off when he heard Sandy say, "Guess who this is?" and he decided he wanted to stick around to hear the lieutenant's response.

"It took you this long to find a phone?" asked the lieutenant, his voice just short of a yell.

Sandy controlled the impulse to yell back. "And here I thought you'd be weeping over our demise."

"By the time I heard about it, the fire department had already ascertained there were no bodies."

"No thanks to you. Sir."

"Where are you?"

"How many people knew about that house, Lieutenant?"

"I asked you a question, McGee."

"I don't think I want to say."

She heard a click on the phone and saw that Chance had gone into the bedroom to listen in on the extension. "Hi, Lieutenant, it's me," he said.

"Well, I know you're someplace with two phones. You probably checked into the Fontainebleau and expect the department to foot the bill."

"How did they get on to us?" asked Sandy.

She could hear Wainger's sigh. "You think I'm not asking myself that?"

"How many people knew?"

"Kelso drove you to the mall, but he didn't know about the house. I suppose he could've followed you, though."

"Nobody followed us," said Chance. "I was looking out for a tail the whole time."

"Who else?" asked Sandy. "Who set up the safe house?"

"I know who set it up, and that's all that matters," said Wainger. "And the next one only I will know about."

"The witness thinks he'd be safer on his own," said Sandy, giving Johnny a look, where he was standing by the door.

"I can't blame him for thinking that," said Wainger. "I've got to admit, we weren't expecting a bomb."

"Neither were we," said Chance.

"I've got another place set up for you," said the lieutenant. "Tight security. It belongs to my rich brother-in-law, who only uses it in the winter."

"Where?" asked Sandy.

"Turnberry Isle."

"You've got to be kidding," she said. "That place is notorious for all the rich drug dealers who live there. Hell, they're the only ones who can afford it."

"Name me a neighborhood in Miami that doesn't have drug dealers," said Wainger.

Sandy tried but couldn't think of one. "Why don't we fly him out of state?"

"And have an entire plane blown up?" asked Chance.

"You don't even have to tell me when you're going over there," said the lieutenant. "The guard at the gate will be alerted that a Mr. and Mrs. Madrigal are coming. Chance will have to show some ID—"

"I don't have any ID," Chance broke in. "It got blown up along with my gun and my clothes."

"Does anyone have any ID?"

Dead silence.

The lieutenant sighed. "Okay, I'm going to put Lathrop on the gate. You two got any objections to her?"

She was a friend of Sandy's, and Sandy immediately said no.

"What about you, Chance?"

"She the blonde?"

"She's okay, Chance," said Sandy. "She's going to law school at night and wants to be a prosecutor."

"I didn't know that," said the lieutenant. "Does that mean we're going to lose her?"

"Forget I said that," said Sandy.

"Okay, here's what you do," said the lieutenant. "Rent a taxi and let me know when you arrive."

"What about clothes?" asked Chance.

"You're not going to be socializing," said the lieutenant.

"I'm not even getting *in* a taxi without some clothes. I've got boxer shorts, Lieutenant, and that's it."

"Never mind, Lieutenant," said Sandy. "I think we'd be better off shopping on our own before we go there. No one knows where we are now. Unless you're having this call traced."

"I wish *I* had thought of that," said Lieutenant Wainger.

Sandy heard Chance hang up, and she followed suit. She'd apologize about that to the lieutenant later.

Sandy showered and dressed in a long, flowered skirt and a black cotton tank top. She put on lipstick and blew her hair dry until it looked fluffy and pretty. Of course, the humidity would soon take care of that, but she'd be damned if she was going to look like a twelve-year-old boy when they saw her next.

Chance leered when she made her appearance, and even Johnny gave a smile of approval. "I'm going shopping, guys," she said, "to get you some clothes."

"We'll all go," said Chance.

"Maybe you can get away with bare feet," said Sandy, "but you can't get away with no pants. Now, tell me what you want and I'll make a list."

"Who's paying for this?" asked Chance.

"The department," said Sandy, trying to sound very sure.

"These jeans will do me," said Johnny, "but I could use some white T-shirts. Preferably all cotton and size large, in case they shrink."

"I'm tired of seeing you in white T-shirts," said Sandy. "Don't you ever wear anything else?"

He eyed her top. "I guess you could get me a black one."

She looked at his bare feet. "Are you married to Reeboks?"

He grinned. "Any sneakers will do," he said. "Size ten."

"Where are you shopping?" asked Chance.

"Don't give me a hard time, Madrigal. I'm not going to the mall, just to a men's store down the street.

And I'm not going to get you any of those slinky shirts you wear open to the waist, either. Just tell me what size pants and shoes.''

"You don't like the way I dress?" Chance asked her, looking hurt.

"You dress like a gigolo," she told him.

"The word is sexy," he corrected her.

"I stand by my first assessment," she said.

Chance looked indignant. "What do you think, Johnny, do I dress like a gigolo?"

"More like a pimp," said Johnny, grinning.

"Well, the hell with you two," said Chance. "You like that understated look? I happen to like a little style."

As soon as she left, Johnny took the dog out in the yard for some exercise and Chance made a phone call. He made it in the kitchen, where he could keep an eye on Johnny.

"Guess who this is?" he asked when he got Rivera, stealing Sandy's line.

A pause, then, "I didn't figure I'd hear from you," said Rivera, having the smarts to sound worried.

"I hope you've got a good explanation, Rivera."

"What can I tell you? The boys got carried away. To show my goodwill, I'll let you decide their punishment.''

"I think you're playing games with me."

"I swear to God, Chance, they were only supposed to hit the bedroom."

"Which bedroom?"

"The one with the bunk beds. They'd already cased the place, and they saw he was sleeping there."

"Yeah? Well, for your information, we were both sleeping there last night. And I was the one you almost got."

"Oh, my God . . ."

"Yeah, that's right, you better start praying."

"I'll make it up to you, I swear. Where are you now?"

"None of your business."

"I still say you ought to do it yourself. That way you have control of things."

"Why the hell can't you just take him out in court?"

"It's not that easy."

"It's easier to bomb a *house*?"

"That wasn't easy, either. You gonna keep in touch?"

"I'll think about it."

"Think about a hundred big ones, Chance."

"*Big ones?* You talking about ten thousand dollars?"

He heard a hoarse laugh. "I'm talking a hundred thou."

"You serious?"

"Dead serious."

Chance began to reassess the situation.

It felt good to get away from them for a little while. She felt a wonderful sense of freedom. Everything seemed so normal in Coconut Grove: tourists crowded the streets; sidewalk cafés were doing good business; clouds were settling in for the usual afternoon rain. She could call Annie, have her meet her for lunch, and never go back to the cottage. Chance and Johnny could take care of themselves.

Except they probably couldn't, particularly with no clothes.

She walked to the end of the block where the men's store was. As soon as she walked in she wanted to buy everything in sight. Chance would look wonderful in that denim vest with the fringe around the arm holes to show off his muscles, and Johnny would look handsome and mysterious in a white linen suit and a straw hat. They'd look good enough to take out and show off, only that was one thing she'd never be allowed to do.

If the salesman wondered at her picking out men's clothing in two different sizes, he didn't say anything. In fact, he tried to sell her more and more, as though she were on some mindless buying spree.

On the way home she stopped and bought herself an ice cream cone, then, feeling guilty, stopped at a bakery and bought chocolate chip cookies for the guys. She found herself eager to get back, forgetting the sense of freedom she had felt only a short time ago. It was her home she wanted to get to, she told herself, only she knew it wasn't just her cottage and Jackson and Fidel. It was also Chance and Johnny—especially Johnny—and she didn't know when that had happened, or how, but the whole idea of it scared her to death.

When she got back they were out in the yard. Chance was in the hammock resting his eyes, and Johnny was playing with Fidel. Or rather, Fidel was playing while Johnny was trying to teach him a trick. She could have told him it was useless.

She handed Johnny the bag of cookies, and he opened the bag, then smiled up at her.

"What's in there?" asked Chance.

"Chocolate chip cookies," she said.

"Where's mine?"

"You can share them, Chance. I got two dozen."

She had bought the usual black pants for Chance, but in a size larger than he had specified. She had been right about that, because they fit him perfectly without showing off every bulge. She'd also bought him some open-necked knit shirts in several pastel colors. She should have guessed he'd pick the lavender one to put on.

She bought them both Reeboks, Chance's in black and Johnny's in white. Johnny had immediately rubbed them in the garden to dirty them up.

She handed out disposable razors and shaving cream, plastic combs and her pièce de résistance, a handgun for Chance.

"Where'd you get that?" Chance asked her.

"I walked into a store and bought it, like everyone else in Florida. Just don't lose this one."

She had also bought—and she was hoping she'd get this past the department's accounting office—three matching terry-cloth robes in navy blue. She hadn't bothered with underwear. It seemed too personal, and she figured they could wash theirs out every night.

"You sure you don't want your head shaved?" she asked Johnny.

"Quite sure."

"You're not going to make a very good impression in court with a ponytail."

"I'll risk it."

"You act like you're Samson or something."

He grinned. "If you shave yours, I'll shave mine."

Chance broke up over that one, which wasn't surprising, since it was exactly the kind of thing he would have said. From Johnny, she was a little surprised.

"Is this luxury or is this decadence?" asked Sandy, walking through the condominium. The outside of Turnberry Isle, with its yacht-filled dock, tennis courts and pool, impeccable landscaping and gracious grounds, had been impressive enough. The condo was downright stunning.

"Luxury," said Chance, wandering down the hallway.

"Pure decadence," said Johnny, but he didn't look displeased.

She opened the doors to the terrace and stepped outside. The terrace was larger than her entire cottage and had a view of the pool, and beyond it, the Intracoastal Waterway. It didn't even seem as hot in Turnberry, as if they had somehow managed to air-condition the outdoors. The condo was furnished with white wrought iron furniture with blue-and-white-striped cushions and an umbrella on the table to match. Potted palm trees blocked the view of the next terrace. There was no barbecue, though. She guessed people with this kind of money didn't grill out.

Johnny came out and stood beside her. "This looks like something in a movie," he said, and she won-

dered if it was for things like this that he had gone
crooked.

"Back inside," she ordered him. "We don't want
you being seen."

As they went in, Chance wandered back. "There're
three bedrooms," he said, "each with its own bath.
And mine has a hot tub."

"Yours?" asked Sandy.

"You're welcome to join me."

Sandy ignored him and went to the kitchen to check
it out. It had a terra cotta floor and cabinets painted
turquoise, a glass table that would seat twelve and
every conceivable appliance, plus a few she had never
seen before. It also had an empty refrigerator.

"They have a great restaurant here," said Chance,
looking over her shoulder into the empty refrigerator.
"We can order in."

"We can also order groceries," said Sandy.

"Oh, come on, let's live it up," he said.

"And just when I was getting used to good home
cooking," said Johnny.

"There's a room back there you'd like, Sandy," said
Chance. "It has wall-to-wall books. What's even better, though, is that it has a pool table."

She saw a light go on in Johnny's eyes. "I wouldn't
mind a game of pool."

The two men disappeared down the hall, and Sandy
checked out the bedrooms. Chance was welcome to
the one with the hot tub. It had silver walls that re-
flected almost as well as a mirror and a black fur
spread on the bed. Even the carpeting on the floor felt
like fur, thick and soft and as black as the spread.
Over the bed was a painting of a topless woman

standing on top of a horse. The whole place gave her the creeps, and she wondered at the lieutenant's brother-in-law's taste.

A second bedroom had a canopy bed rather like her own and was all done up in pink. It had a dressing table with ruffles and pictures of ballerinas on the walls. It looked like a young girl's bedroom, and she decided it would be funny to relegate Johnny to that one.

The third bedroom was all white—walls, tile floor, wicker furniture, bedspread, everything. The only touch of color came from the plants in front of the French doors. It also had its own terrace. She put her suitcase on the bed and began to unpack.

She was starting to feel safe here: Jill Lathrop was on the gate for the duration; there was an excellent security system, complete with burglar alarm; and four private security guards the lieutenant had hired were keeping a watch on their building. Plus they were on the top floor, with no easy way to shoot through their windows. It sure beat being in a ranch house in Miami Shores. If she could have brought Fidel and Jackson along, it would have been perfect.

She put her clothes away and wandered down to where the guys were to look over the books. They were so intent on their game they hardly noticed her as she browsed through the bookcases. There were books of all kinds; she wouldn't run out of reading material here. She also liked pool, but she'd wait until later to spring that on them. They both looked as though they needed some practice before playing her. Thanks to her dad, she was something of a pool shark.

And speaking of pools... "Do you guys think it would be okay if I went down for a swim?"

"Sure, go on," said Chance. "That way maybe you'll let me take advantage of their health club later. I'd like to lift a few weights while I have the opportunity."

"Anyone for tennis?" asked Johnny.

"You don't get to go out," said Sandy. "Sorry."

"I was just kidding," he said. "I hate tennis. I wouldn't mind a swim, though."

"Maybe Chance will let you into his hot tub."

"Did you see the size of the TV screen?" Chance asked her.

"I would have had to be blind not to see it. It practically takes up an entire wall. What I like is the central air-conditioning. We could actually wear sweatshirts in here and never know it was summer."

She put on her bathing suit and took the elevator down to the pool area. Several anorexic-looking blondes were lounging beside it, and they all ignored her. Good. If they were snobbish, she wouldn't have to make up a story for them.

She dived into the warm water and started to swim the length of the pool. What had earlier felt like a hot, humid nasty kind of day, now began to seem perfect. Maybe money could buy happiness after all.

In a setting of such sheer perfection, she was sure nothing bad could possibly happen.

Chapter 6

This is a nice place, Lieutenant.''

"A little rich for my blood, McGee, but glad you like it.''

Reggae music suddenly blasted out of the CD player. "Turn it down!" Sandy shouted at Chance.

The music was turned down to a roar, and she walked down the hall with the phone. It was the kind that didn't need to be plugged in, and she loved it already. She ended up in one of the bathrooms and closed the door behind her to shut out the noise.

"So how's it going, McGee?''

"So far so good. The place seems as impregnable as possible, under the circumstances, but I still don't like the idea of a leak.''

"I'm looking into that. How's the witness?''

"Well, he's a pretty fair poker player and a hotshot at pool. He's also not a bad cook.''

"Sounds like the perfect man."

"We're getting along all right. He's not so bad. Easier to get along with than Madrigal, actually."

"That's why I made you partners," said the lieutenant. "A little friction between partners is a good thing. Keeps you on your toes."

"Maybe during an eight-hour shift, but round the clock it gets tiresome."

"Keep alert, McGee, that's all I'm asking. Don't let anyone in the door unless it's me, and it's not going to be me. Something else—if it's not a leak, I think we can assume you're safe."

"On what evidence?"

"We had the fire department put it out to the papers that three bodies were found in the house."

"That would sound good if it weren't for the fact that if it wasn't a leak, how did they find us?"

"Someone could've followed the Feds."

"I hope you're right, Lieutenant."

"Yeah, so do I."

"Hey, Sandy, come out here," yelled Chance from the terrace.

She walked out to a spectacular view of the sunset.

"Nice, huh?" he asked.

"Very nice."

"I could get used to this, you know what I mean?"

He meant they were being spoiled by the luxury, and she felt it, too.

"Come over here by me," he said, his voice entreating.

"Forget it."

He lowered his voice. "It's not going to hurt for the neighbors to see a happy couple out here. They could be wondering about us, you know."

She looked around and saw a few other people out on their terraces enjoying the view. He had a point— a self-serving point, but a point nonetheless. She went over and stood beside him and didn't object when he put his arm around her waist.

"Smile, at least," he muttered.

She smiled and leaned her head against his shoulder. What the hell, he wasn't that bad at times.

"What do you think a place like this costs, McGee?"

"More than we'll ever be able to afford."

"Speak for yourself. I could win the lottery any day now."

"It's for damn sure you're not going to get rich from poker. Or hustling pool, by the looks of it."

"You're not going to let me forget you beat me, are you?"

"No."

"You're a hard woman, McGee."

"You're a lousy pool player."

"Tell me the truth, wouldn't you like to live in a place like this?"

"Not really."

"You're lying, McGee."

"I'm not saying I wouldn't like to be able to afford it, but I don't like planned communities. I'd rather have one of those old houses in Coral Gables, or a Victorian house in Key West."

"Not me, I like all this high-tech luxury."

"This place isn't decorated in high tech."

"No?"

"No."

"What about all those electronic toys?"

"Okay, so they have a few toys."

"They have ones I never even heard of."

"You could probably get a hot tub put in your apartment."

"It wouldn't be the same. It would take up the entire bathroom. You ought to try it, McGee. You don't know what you're missing."

"Let's go inside. We shouldn't be leaving Johnny alone," she said.

"Johnny's okay—he's in the hot tub. Unless you were itching to join him, if you get my meaning."

"What's it like?"

"Great. Relaxing. All these jets of water shoot out on you. You gotta try it. It's even fun alone."

"Is there a lock on the door?"

He laughed, catching her off guard for a moment, so that when he moved in and put his arms around her, she couldn't get away. When his mouth closed over hers, she didn't make a fuss, didn't even squirm. She just closed it tightly and waited him out.

It only took him a few seconds to concede defeat. He let go of her and put on his boyish smile, looking around. "Well, the neighbors enjoyed it, anyway."

"Don't try it again," she warned him.

"Or what? You'll throw me across the terrace?"

"I'll throw you *off* the terrace."

He laughed at her. "So I'm not a black belt. You really think I need it against you? Hell, I must have fifty pounds on you."

"More like seventy-five," she needled him.

"You telling me I'm putting on weight?"

"At the rate you're eating, I'd start working out if I were you."

"You're right, I'm getting out of shape. You mind if I go down to the health club and lift a few?"

"Not at all," said Sandy. Maybe he could work off his sexual frustration at the same time.

Random had thought she was going to come out of the clinch swinging, but they seemed amiable enough out there—that was good. He didn't want bad feelings between the two. Forced to be together all the time, it could only cause trouble. To be honest, though, he'd been hoping she'd belt Chance one.

Chance came into the room saying, "I'm going down to the health club for a while. Maybe we could get permission from the lieutenant for you to go down there with me, Johnny."

"Thanks," said Random, "but I don't work out."

"Never? How do you stay in shape?"

"I run."

"Yeah, you look like a runner. How'd you like the hot tub?"

Random couldn't stop the smile. "It was great. I'd like to have one of those."

Sandy came in from the terrace and closed and locked the door. She pulled the curtains across as the last of the sun disappeared. "What would you like to have?" she asked him, going around the room and turning on lamps.

"He wants a hot tub," said Chance. "If you're going to try it, Sandy, do it now, because I'll be wanting to use it again after I work out."

"What're you going to work out in?" Sandy asked him.

"You think you know everything, don't you?" Chance asked her. "It just so happens they have a shop down there that sells workout clothes."

"How do you—"

"Because I used to date a woman who lives here," he said.

"Really?" she asked, a deceptively sweet smile on her face. "And what do you plan on using for money?"

For a moment Chance looked as though he was about to put his foot through the wall. Then he stalked out of the room and disappeared down the hall.

"Why do you keep giving him a hard time?" Random asked her.

She looked surprised. "You think that was a hard time?"

"Yeah, I'd say so."

"I was just getting warmed up."

She started walking around the room, studying the paintings on the wall. He'd been impressed when he first saw them, but he didn't think she had noticed them until now.

"I think these are real," she finally said.

"I think you're right."

"Can you imagine having them in your living room? They should be in a museum."

"I like the O'Keeffe," he said.

"Which one is that?"

"The square one over the bar."

She looked at the O'Keeffe, then gave him a wordless look, probably wondering how a flower could be so sexy.

"You have your place fixed up nice," he said.

She gave him a pleased look. "You think so?"

"I felt comfortable there."

"I've got it just exactly the way I want it."

"It looked like that. It looked like you took care with it."

"I did a lot of work on it, but it was worth it. I like staying home. I'm happy there."

Chance walked into the room wearing gray sweatpants and a tank top with the number forty-nine on it. "See you guys later," he said. "Don't do anything I wouldn't do."

Sandy's mouth dropped open. "Where'd you come up with those?"

Chance shrugged. "They were in the closet." He didn't wait around for an argument, and the front door was closed a moment later.

One thing, Johnny thought. No matter how much the two of them argued, she never seemed ill at ease when Chance was around. But when she was alone with him, she always appeared to be on edge. He tried to ease this by not crowding her.

Right now she was hovering by the door, probably trying to decide if she could protect him from another room.

"You really ought to try it," he told her.

"What?"

"The hot tub."

"I think I'd like to."

"Go on, nothing's stopping you. It takes a while to fill."

She shook her head and walked over to one of the couches and sat down. He was on the one facing her, but there was still a distance of several feet between them and an enormous marble, free-form coffee table in between.

"I better not," she said. "I shouldn't leave you on your own that long."

"Leave me your gun. I can take care of myself."

She looked briefly tempted. "I'll try it before Chance goes to bed."

"If I had gone to the health club with him, you would've been able to use it."

"It's not safe for you to be outside."

"It's funny, but I feel perfectly safe here. It just doesn't seem like the kind of place where anything bad could happen."

"Did you feel safe at the first house?"

He shook his head. "It was too easy to get in that place, and on the ground floor and all."

"And we didn't even have the doors locked."

"Yeah, well, you learned fast."

"We could've gotten you killed."

"Listen, you did just fine. Don't worry about it. Can I interest you in a game of pool?"

"Couldn't we just talk?"

That took him by surprise. "Talk?"

"Tell me about yourself."

"I don't think so, Sandy."

"I'm not asking you anything confidential. Isn't there anything in your life innocent enough to tell me about?"

He thought about it for a few moments and then chuckled. "You want to hear up to the age of ten?"

"No, I want to hear what happened at age ten to make you lose your innocence?"

He grinned. "Pumpkins."

"Pumpkins?"

"We rode our bikes out of town and stole some pumpkins from a farmer. And then we smashed them against the witch's house."

"Right."

"I'm serious. She was this old lady in the neighborhood, and we called her the witch. She ran my dog over with her car and wasn't even sorry about it. I hated her."

"I don't blame you."

"She seemed old. I guess she was probably only in her forties, but she was older than the rest of the mothers, and she always dressed in black. She had this little boy we called the sissy. He just stayed in his front yard, dressed in these little sailor outfits, and referred to himself in the third person. We used to make his life miserable."

"It sounds like his mother was doing that."

"I'd forgotten about that. About my dog. The problem was, he used to chase cars and bark at them. She probably didn't mean to hit him."

"But she wasn't sorry."

He shook his head. "No, she never was. Never came over and apologized or anything."

"That's really sad. Tell me a happy memory."

He took a long time thinking about it. "I was nine when I got my tonsils taken out."

"That's a happy memory?"

"Wait. I get home from the hospital, and my folks had bought me my own color TV for my room. And I got to eat nothing but Jell-O and ice cream for a week."

"Where did you live?"

He hesitated a moment and then decided it didn't matter. "Indiana. You ever been there?"

"No."

"What were you like when you were a kid?"

"I was a sweet, quiet little girl until the third grade."

"What happened in the third grade?"

"I met Annie and Bolivia. Annie was too smart for her own good, and Bolivia was a holy terror. I still played dolls then, but when Bolivia found out, she made me kill them off and bury them in the backyard. Then she taught me how to play baseball."

"I can't even remember the names of my friends in the third grade."

"They're still my friends. And we still play baseball together."

"They live around here?"

She nodded. "Things are changing, though. Annie got married this summer, and Bolivia fell in love. She won't admit it, of course, but that's what happened. And now she's over in Beirut with him, and they're probably getting themselves killed."

"Since I'm sure they didn't go to Lebanon on vacation..."

"They're reporters, both of them. And Annie's a lawyer."

"It's good to have close friends."

"Do you have any?" She threw in the question so quickly he almost answered spontaneously.

He forced himself to pause before speaking, and he could see the disappointment on her face. "I guess not," he said.

He thought she'd change the subject, but instead she asked, "I'm not trying to offend you, Johnny, but when you were a kid, did you snitch on other kids."

"No, I didn't, Sandy."

"I always thought that was the worst thing you could do."

"So did I, when I was a kid. But back then it was us against them, and the 'them' were the adults. Things change when you get older."

"I understand that. And I understand that the people you're testifying against deserve to be punished, but I still don't think I could do it."

"You'd rather go to prison?"

"I guess I would."

"You know what it's like in prison?"

"Yes."

"I wouldn't last a day in prison."

"Maybe you should've thought of that—no, I'm sorry. I'm not here to judge you."

"I guess you can't help thinking it."

"Maybe," she said, "but I can help what I talk about."

"Can you see yourself doing anything that could conceivably land you in prison?" he asked.

He watched her as she chewed on her lip, something she seemed to be in the habit of doing whenever she was engaged in serious thought.

"I guess we're all capable of things that could land us in prison," she said. "But it wouldn't be for money, and it wouldn't involve drugs."

Damn, in a minute he was going to be confessing to her. There was something about her that made him want to tell her everything.

"What's the matter, Johnny?"

"That restaurant. How late does it deliver?"

She gave him a disappointed look, as though she had been expecting him to say something else. "Eleven, I think."

"You think we could order up some iced tea?"

"I don't see why not. Tomorrow I'm going to get some groceries. We can still order some of our meals, but it's nice to have stuff in the house."

"Maybe we could order a beer for Chance."

"We're not supposed to be drinking on duty."

"He'll be going to bed soon anyway. One beer's not going to do anything to him."

"I suppose you'd like one, too."

"Iced tea's fine."

She got up. "I just love that telephone you can carry around," she said, sounding almost excited about being able to use it again.

Despite the fact she sometimes sounded like a kid, he realized he was long past thinking of her as a midget.

It wasn't half-bad staying up late in a place that had so many things she could amuse herself with. She watched the late news on the giant TV screen, practiced a little pool, used the personal computer to make out a grocery list and would have used the FAX machine if she had been able to figure it out. She even inspected the condo every half hour, checking all the doors and windows and making sure the terrace was empty, and then looking in on Johnny and Chance.

She was well into a book when Chance came out to relieve her. She was surprised he had woken up on his own.

"Everything quiet?" he asked.

"Well, I haven't heard any bombs going off."

"Don't even *say* that!"

She looked up at him. "You look like you're going to fall asleep again."

"I'm okay. They have all the cable channels here. I'm going to watch me some blue movies."

She was about to make a smart remark, then realized that that was probably the only thing guaranteed to keep him awake.

"I'm going to do some grocery shopping in the morning."

"By telephone."

"I don't want to do it by telephone. I like to see what I'm getting."

"Since we don't have any money and we don't have a car, I think you better let the lieutenant take care of it."

"I have money. Who do you think paid for dinner?"

"I figured you charged it to the apartment number."

"This isn't a hotel. I brought my checkbook and some money with me from home."

"Then you could've bought me some workout clothes."

"Keep dreaming, Madrigal."

He reached out a hand and tousled her hair. "Go to bed, kid—you didn't get much sleep last night."

"I'm going to use the hot tub first."

He grinned. "Is that a thinly-veiled invitation?"

"God, Madrigal, don't you ever give it up?"

"Never!" he called out to her as she left the room.

The hot tub was even better than the telephone. In fact, there was a telephone on the wall right next to it. Which wasn't surprising, as there seemed to be a telephone in every room in the condo. Either the owners were lazy or they liked to talk on the phone a lot.

She was tempted to pick up the phone and call someone and say, "Hey, you'll never believe where I'm calling from—a hot tub." Only who did you call with that kind of information at four in the morning?

She could see why the guys were crazy about it. She couldn't remember ever feeling so relaxed, and the jets of warm water felt sexy when they hit her breasts. Which wasn't something she should be thinking about at all when she was locked up in an apartment with what were probably two horny men. At least, one of them was; Chance was perpetually horny. And Johnny probably hadn't had a woman—

Why was she thinking about things like that?

She had heard of couples using hot tubs. Well, she'd also heard of groups, but she was pretty sure that was only done in California. Probably by movie stars.

She could see where it wouldn't be so bad, though, being in a hot tub with some man you were crazy about. There sure was plenty of room. Not too much room, of course, but just enough. They'd be touching, but not really crowding each other.

She leaned back and rested her head on the ledge and closed her eyes. And then, without even consciously thinking about it, a picture formed of her and Johnny in the hot tub together. She was so shocked she opened her eyes and sat up straight. In a hot tub with a crooked cop? A crooked cop who was a *snitch*? What was the matter with her? Was she losing all her ethical values being around the two of them?

She shouldn't be in a hot tub. Where she should be was in a cold shower.

How do you play poker with a guy, shoot some games of pool with him, talk a little sports, trade stories about old girlfriends, and then set him up to be killed? He hadn't gone into it to get people killed, damn it. What he was doing wasn't any better than hiring out as an assassin. And if Rivera sent the same slobs to do the job the second time, there was sure no guarantee that he and Sandy wouldn't buy it, either.

Damn it anyway! Naked people all over the giant screen—naked people so life-size they looked like they were in the same room with him, like he could join in the orgy by just getting up—and he couldn't even concentrate on the damn movie.

Why had he joined the force in the first place? He could have circumvented all this to begin with if he'd just gone straight into the drug trade. It wouldn't have been hard to do. He'd had the right connections. But no, he had to be the big law and order one in those days. Lost half his friends when he joined the force, but he hadn't cared. So what if they were getting rich? They were getting killed, too.

Okay, so he'd thought he was making his mother happy. Maybe she would've been happier with an apartment like this and a charge account at Saks. Maybe she would have liked being driven around in her son's limousine and having someone to clean her house instead of having to clean other people's houses. So now he had some extra money, and she wouldn't even take it. He tried to give her some, but she'd refused it, telling him to save it for when he got married. And when he offered to buy her a car, she told him she was too old to learn to drive, and anyway, the drivers in Miami were crazy.

He didn't even have anything to show for it. All the extra money he pulled in went for his gambling debts. Which should probably tell him something, only it wasn't like he was addicted to gambling or anything like that. It was what he did for fun, that's all, and he spent an equal amount of time working out. There were women, too, but how much time did women take? Not a hell of a lot when they were the kind of women he didn't exactly want to talk to.

The thing is, how could he *not* call Rivera? This wasn't something he could just walk away from, telling Rivera he had changed his mind and decided to go straight. He'd be dead the next minute. He could run. He could get out of the country. But it took money to get out of the country, and there wasn't any guarantee they wouldn't find him anyway. Rivera probably had connections all over the world. At least, any place he'd want to go to. Sure, he could go to some place like Denmark, but he didn't even know where it was exactly, and the only things he knew for sure about it were that the women were blond and the weather was cold. He could handle the blondes all right, but he sure as hell couldn't handle the cold.

A hundred thou. What could he do with a hundred thou? Just about anything, he guessed. He wouldn't even gamble it away; he could invest in the stock market or something, make his money grow. He wondered if they took cash. Hell, they must take cash, Rivera and his buddies all played the market.

He got up and walked down the hall. Sandy was sleeping like a baby, all curled up in that big white bed. He wondered how she'd liked the hot tub. Down the hall Johnny was talking in his sleep. He guessed that came of having something on his conscience. He was a good guy, though, not the type Chance would've expected to get involved in the drug business. He seemed intelligent and talked like he'd gotten some education and gone to some schools. Chance didn't know why someone like that would join the force in the first place.

Back in the living room, he left the TV on and picked up the phone. So it was five in the morning, so what? Rivera should be glad he even bothered to call.

For once Rivera picked up the phone himself.

"Guess who?" said Chance.

"Good to hear from you, *compadre*."

And wasn't Rivera sounding unusually friendly at five in the a.m. "I'm going to give it to you straight, Rivera."

"I'm listening."

"I wrote out a confession. For my own protection, you know what I mean?"

A pause, then, "Go on."

"Just in case something happens to me. I mailed it to someone I can trust."

"It was a foul-up, Chance. Hell, you've been more help to me than any ten guys you can name. I was thinking about it tonight and figured you've saved me millions."

"Millions?"

"You've been a big help."

"And so you're going to reward me with a lousy hundred thou?"

"You get greedy in this business, Madrigal—"

"Don't talk greedy to *me*, Rivera. I'm not the one living in a mansion with my own private jet and a yacht docked out front."

"I'm sure we can work something out."

"Now."

"I like a good businessman. Here's my proposition. We up it to five for information, a million if you do the job yourself."

It took Chance a moment to realize that a million wasn't going to do him a hell of a lot of good in prison. "Five sounds about right. Here's the set up, but it's not going to be easy."

"Nothing worthwhile ever is," said Rivera, his voice more seductive than what was going on on the screen.

Chapter 7

Sandy was fixing lunch, and Johnny was putting away the groceries that had just been delivered. Chance was working out and due back any minute.

She was feeling a little nervous being alone with Johnny. Not that he purposely did anything to make her nervous, but she still couldn't get the picture of the two of them in the hot tub out of her mind. She'd be thinking about something else, and then she'd look at him, and it would spring back.

She tried to think when the last time was that she'd had any kind of a relationship with a man, but the only one she could remember was Greg Martin, and that had been a good three years ago. God, had it been that long? No wonder her friends were always trying to fix her up with men.

"Tuna salad okay with you?" she asked him, thinking it wouldn't do any of them any harm to cut down on the calories. They were all eating like they were on a vacation cruise, which wasn't a bad analogy: they were stuck in one place, they were getting bored and food was something to look forward to.

"I'm not fussy," said Johnny, reaching up to put the spices on the top shelf.

"Well, I am, and I wish you wouldn't put food in the top cupboard where I can't reach it."

He grinned. "You have two able-bodied men to get it down for you."

"I like being self-sufficient."

"I've noticed."

There was something in his voice that made her ask, "What else have you noticed?"

She thought he was about to reply, but then she heard the front door slam and voices in the hallway. *Voices?* She was about to reach for her gun, which was stuffed into her waistband and covered by the apron, when she realized that one of the voices was female.

Chance and a young, pretty, very tall blonde came into the kitchen, both of them still laughing at something.

Sandy looked at Johnny, but he was behaving normally, and she decided she'd better, too, until she found out what was up. And the explanation had better be good.

"Hi, guys," said Chance. "This is Michelle. I met her down at the health club. Michelle, this is my sister, Sandy, and her husband, Johnny, who are visiting me from the Big Apple."

"I just love New York," said Michelle, leaning into Johnny as though they'd known each other for ages.

"They just got married," said Chance with a wicked smile. "I try to give them as much time alone as possible, if you get my meaning."

Michelle giggled.

"Michelle's a stewardess." Chance made it sound like the career opportunity of a lifetime.

"We're called flight attendants now," Michelle corrected him.

Okay, so this wasn't regulation behavior on his part. Sandy thought she ought to make the best of it. She was sure that even Johnny wasn't finding Michelle a threat to his life. "Are you staying for lunch?" she asked the young woman.

"I never eat," said Michelle, "but I'll keep you company."

Johnny and Michelle sat down at the table. Sandy had a feeling Chance would rather get Michelle into the hot tub than have lunch, but that wasn't going to be easy, with her and Johnny there.

Sandy carried the tuna salad over to the table. "You want me to get the iced tea, darling?" Johnny asked her.

Sandy tried to control the laugh, but it burst out anyway. "That would be nice, sweetheart," she replied, hearing Johnny laughing now, too.

"What's so funny?" asked Michelle.

"Damned if I know," said Chance. "The two of them laugh over anything. I guess it's love."

"That's sweet," said Michelle.

"Yeah, but it makes me feel left out."

"Well, I'll try to make up for that," whispered Michelle, loud enough for everyone to hear.

Sandy rolled her eyes and looked at Johnny, who seemed to be amused by the situation.

"I love your apartment," said Michelle.

"Thanks," said Chance. "I bought it furnished."

"It's really nice. All we have so far is some mattresses on the floor."

"You don't live alone?" Sandy asked her.

Michelle shook her head. "I share with five other flight attendants. We thought it would be worth the rent to live here 'cause we figured we'd meet lots of guys with money. So far, though, they're all old, and they all have wives."

"Your luck has changed," said Chance with a sexy grin.

"I guess it has," agreed Michelle. "I think I'm going to keep you away from my roommates, though. They can find their own men."

After lunch Chance said, "Want to help me clean up, Michelle, and give them some time alone together?"

"That won't be necessary," said Sandy.

"Go on," said Chance. "Why don't you guys take a nap or something?"

"Can I see you for a moment in the living room, brother dear?" asked Sandy.

As soon as she got him alone she said, "Get rid of her!"

"Hey, she's not hurting anything. Listen, I already searched her for bombs."

"The lieutenant wouldn't like this, Madrigal."

"So who's gonna tell him?"

"I wanted to go down and have a swim this afternoon. I could use some exercise, too, you know."

"So who's stopping you? Michelle and I will baby-sit Johnny."

"What if she wants to go out with you? What're you going to tell her?"

"She won't mind staying home. Hell, we have everything here."

Sandy gave up and went back to the kitchen, where Michelle was telling Johnny about all the places she had flown to.

Chance stuck his head in and said, "Hey, Michelle, I'll show you around the place." She was out of the kitchen without completing her sentence.

"She's okay," said Johnny, carrying the dishes over to the sink.

"I have nothing against her," said Sandy. "It's Chance doing a thing like that that bothers me. He shouldn't even be going to the health club, but picking up women?"

"It'll get him off your back for a while."

"Yeah, there's that," she agreed.

When the hot water she was filling the sink with suddenly turned cold, she swore.

"What's the matter?" Johnny asked her.

Sandy turned off the water and listened. "Damn it, they're in the hot tub."

Johnny chuckled. "I could've predicted that."

"Can you believe it? They've only known each other an hour."

"You've got to watch out for blondes. They move fast."

She was about to argue with him when he said, "Hey, I'm only kidding."

"That sounded like something Chance would say."

"I figured I'd fill in for him."

"Don't do me any favors."

"So, my dear bride, what are we going to do this afternoon?"

"What I wanted to do was take a swim, but I guess that's going to have to wait."

"I really can look out for myself, you know. I've probably been a cop longer than you."

"And I can do without a swim."

"But you shouldn't have to."

"What about some more chess lessons?"

"It would be my pleasure, but hardly believable. I don't think I've ever heard of people playing chess on their honeymoon."

"You act like we have to convince her. Michelle wasn't suspicious. And if she were, you being in protective custody would be the last thing that would occur to her. Anyway, not everyone spends their honeymoon in a hot tub."

"No, that wouldn't be my first choice," said Johnny, and she wished she hadn't even mentioned the hot tub. Now that picture was flashing in her mind again—in living color, no less.

"What's the matter?" he asked, and she realized she must be blushing.

"Nothing."

"All right, chess it is, but be sure to sprinkle in a few endearments."

"I'm going to sprinkle more than endearments over your head in a minute."

"I always said men were the romantics."

"I always thought I was a romantic," said Sandy. "I guess I'm growing out of it."

"Or you're losing it through disuse."

She glanced up at him. "You're pretty perceptive."

"I just know that it's happening to me."

Sandy took off the apron and hung it on a hook. She was about to tell him that she'd like to water the house plants first when she heard what sounded like a chime.

"What's that, the phone?" she asked, but Johnny was already on his way down the hall.

"What is it?" she asked, running after him.

"I think it's the door," he said.

She caught up with him and blocked his way. "For God's sake, don't answer it."

"I wasn't going to. I'll be behind the door, though, if you need some help."

"You think I should answer it? No one gets in here without going through the gate first, which means they should have called us."

"Believe me, Sandy, these aren't the kind of people who are going to announce themselves at the gate."

The chime sounded again.

The door had a peephole, and Sandy stood on her toes to look through it. All she could see was a gray blur.

"Who is it?" she yelled through the door.

"Building maintenance, ma'am."

"What should I do?" she asked Johnny.

"I think we should get Chance."

"Fat lot of good he is, in the damn hot tub."

She drew her gun and opened the door, holding the gun behind the door so that it wouldn't be seen. Two Hispanic men stood there, both of them in gray uniforms with "Turnberry" embroidered over the pockets of their shirts. "May I see some identification?" she asked them.

The two men looked confused. The smaller one said, "*What* identification? We're here because the apartment below you has a leak coming through their ceiling."

"I'm going to have to check you out with the office," she said, starting to close the door.

"You don't have time for that," said the larger of the two, pushing against the door and flattening it against Johnny.

Without even thinking Sandy grabbed the man and flipped him over on his back, then held her gun on the other one. "Call the police, Johnny."

"What the hell, you crazy, lady?" asked the smaller man, looking bug-eyed at her gun.

"Turn around and put your hands on the railing," she ordered him, and when he did what she said, she jabbed the other man with her foot. "Get up and do the same," she told him. "And don't make any wrong moves."

The man was swearing at her in Spanish, probably figuring she didn't know the language. She told him in Spanish that if he wanted a bullet in his back, to just keep talking.

She saw Johnny in the doorway. "I told you to call the police," she practically screamed at him.

A crowd was gathering down by the pool, all of them looking up to where they stood on the balcony. "*Now*, Johnny!"

"I think they're building maintenance," he said. "I've seen them before."

"You couldn't have seen them."

"I saw them out the window when they were painting the building trim."

She asked the men their names, and when they told her, she told Johnny to hold the gun on them while she called the gate.

Five minutes later the men had checked out and she felt like a fool.

"Sorry," she said to them as she told them they could turn around.

"You still got a leak," the larger one said to her, but his voice was respectful. "Probably the hot tub. It's happened before."

Sandy smiled. "The hot tub? Oh, well, go right in and take care of it. I'd hate for our hot tub to be causing a leak."

Ten seconds later girlish screams could be heard from down the hall.

"That was mean," said Johnny, but he was grinning.

"I know, but he deserved it. He should've been out here." She shoved the gun back into her waistband. "I feel really stupid. We're supposed to keep a low profile, and the whole building's seen me flashing my gun."

"I thought you were great."

"Hardly my best performance."

"Throwing him on his back with just your left arm, that was pretty impressive."

She heard Chance and Michelle in the hallway, and from the sound of Chance's voice he was furious.

"Kiss me," said Johnny.

She looked at him and saw the wicked gleam in his eyes. She saw the opportunity to put a joke over on

Chance and moved into Johnny's arms, turning her face up to meet his kiss. Even before his mouth met hers she felt shaken, and she guessed it was the aftermath of the excitement. Action always did get the adrenaline stirring. But the joke on Chance was turning into a joke on her.

"What the hell?" came the thunder of Chance's voice. "Will someone please explain to me—"

Sandy broke off the kiss and turned to her partner, who was clothed only in a towel around his waist. "What's the matter, brother dear?"

"And what the hell do you think *you're* doing?" he asked them.

Sandy winked at Michelle, who was wearing one of the navy blue robes, and smiled at Chance. "Just enjoying my honeymoon."

Johnny took advantage of the situation by keeping an arm around her. "It looks like you two were in the hot tub," he said to Chance.

Chance looked slightly flustered. "What about it?"

"Nothing," said Johnny. "I guess it's a good way to get to know each other."

"You telling me what I can do in my own house?"

"We were just about to play chess," said Sandy, with a perky smile for both of them. "Maybe you two would like to watch."

Chance turned around and grabbed Michelle by the hand. "Chess. Can you believe? What kind of people would play chess on their honeymoon?"

"Not me," said Michelle, disappearing down the hall with him.

"Not me, either," said Johnny.

Sandy decided it was unanimous.

* * *

"We're in charge of dinner," Chance had said, and Sandy knew that meant he was ordering in. That was okay with her; she didn't feel like cooking for four anyway, and Michelle didn't seem about to leave. Surprisingly, though, things were better between the three of them with Michelle around. It helped to reduce the tension to pretend to be ordinary people for a while.

What Sandy hadn't counted on, though, was Chance setting up a table for two for the honeymooners, complete with candlelight, in the living room, and he and Michelle eating alone in the kitchen. Romantic music was wafting through the air from the stereo.

She was about to issue a voluble protest when Johnny caught her eye and shook his head. "Don't," he whispered.

"I don't see why—"

"I wouldn't mind a meal alone with you."

She knew what he meant. Michelle and Chance had reached the stage where they were all over each other, making Johnny and Sandy look like the most unromantic honeymooning couple of all time.

Sandy made a couple of changes, though. She blew out the candles, opened the blinds and turned the radio to a rock station. It wasn't even dark yet, for heaven's sake.

"Steak again," she said, seating herself at the table.

"We really ought to complain," he said. "There are millions of people out there who don't get steak every night."

She started to smile. "And millions more starving."

He grinned. "Exactly."

"But no wine. If he really wanted to do it up right, he would've had wine."

"What do you want to bet he's got wine out there for them?"

"Don't even say that, Johnny. Don't make me have to get up and go out there and check on him. No, he couldn't possibly do something that stupid."

He lifted his glass of ice water as though to toast. "To a quiet few days at Turnberry," he said, his eyes looking into hers.

She loved the way an edge of black circled his soft green irises. He had the prettiest eyes she'd seen outside of a few cats.

"I'll drink to that," she said.

She liked his table manners, too. Unlike Chance, who thought eating consisted of putting his face as close to the plate as he could manage and wolfing down the food as though someone were about to snatch it away from him, Johnny ate slowly and seemed to savor every bite. She wondered if there was any correlation between the way a man ate and the way he made love. Of course, if that extended to women, it would make her a nibbler.

"What're you thinking about?" he asked.

"You had to wait until the one exact moment when I'm thinking something I shouldn't be thinking to ask that, didn't you?"

"You had a provocative look on your face, and I didn't think it was due to the steak."

She felt herself blushing and wished she had left the blinds closed. He wasn't going to mention it, was he? He wouldn't dare.

He dared. "About before . . ." he said. "After your impressive karate display."

"I don't want to talk about it," she said, quickly putting a big piece of steak in her mouth and hoping he'd follow suit.

"I think we should. It's making you nervous around me, and I'm sorry about that."

"I've always been nervous around you."

"Yes, but this is a different kind of nervousness."

"Don't start something, Johnny, or I'll do the same to you." If he could make her nervous bringing up the kiss, she could reciprocate with talk of the trial.

He smiled. "I know that was meant to scare me, but it didn't work."

She decided not to pick up the challenge.

"It wasn't pretend, Sandy. I wanted to kiss you."

She slammed down her fork and glared at him. Okay, he was asking for it. "How could you do it, Johnny?"

"It was very easy."

"I'm not talking about the kiss. I'm talking about going bad, about snitching on the other cops. I always thought I was a pretty good judge of character, and you're not the type." She caught herself practically yelling toward the end and lowered her voice.

His eyes turned shadowy for a moment, and then he looked down at his plate. She held her breath until he said, "I can't talk about it, Sandy."

"Baloney. You just don't want to talk about it."

He looked up. "That's not true. I'd very much like to talk about it."

"Sure, you want to tell me all the mitigating circumstances. The problem is, there aren't any for something like that."

"Everything's black and white, right?"

"Some things are, yes."

"You don't know anything about this."

"And you won't tell me."

"That's right."

Why did they have to start this during dinner? She wasn't going to find out anything, and she was going to end up with an upset stomach.

"Don't do it again," she said, and knew he understood that it was the kiss she was talking about.

"If I had thought it would turn out that way, I wouldn't have done it in the first place. I mean it. It was just supposed to be a joke on Chance, but then it turned into something else."

"I don't think we ought to analyze it."

"I know you think it's the proximity, or maybe the fact that I'm just an all-out bastard. You're wrong. I'm starting to care about you."

"If you don't stop it, I'm going to go out and eat with Chance and Michelle."

"I'm not coming on to you. I just wanted you to know how I feel."

"I don't want you starting to care about me."

"I'm sorry, it's too late."

"Listen, John Doe—I'm here to guard you and nothing else."

"It won't happen again. I know the circumstances aren't right, and it would complicate the situation we're in, but at least admit you feel the same."

She stared him in the eye and lied through her teeth. "I'm sorry, Johnny, but I don't care about you. You look good at times when compared to Chance, but I really hate what you are."

She didn't know what she'd expected, maybe a show of remorse, but he surprised her by laughing. "Maybe you're fooling yourself, but you're not fooling me."

There was a sudden thump behind her that must have come from the terrace. In a flash she was up, shoving Johnny to the floor and knocking the table over in the process. She drew her gun and threw herself between him and the sliding glass doors, the gun aimed at the glass.

There was dead silence for a moment, and then he said, "It was a volleyball."

She couldn't have heard him correctly. "What?"

He cleared his throat, and it sounded as though he was trying not to laugh. "A volleyball landed on the terrace, orange and white striped. Someone must have made a bad shot from the pool."

She looked at the remains of their dinner strewn all over the white wall-to-wall carpeting. She slowly got to her feet and walked over to the terrace. The ball was sitting there, just as he had said.

She opened the terrace door and stepped outside. She picked up the ball, looked down at the pool and saw a group of teenage boys looking up at her. She tossed them the ball.

"Thanks, lady," one of them yelled out.

She went back inside and closed the door. Johnny was cleaning up the mess.

"You can't say my reactions aren't quick," she said, feeling stupid for the second time that day.

"All this nervous energy of yours could be used in more creative ways," he said, a wicked gleam in his eyes.

"Will you quit sounding like Chance?"

He set the plates back on the table. "Come here."

She backed up. "Stay away from me."

"I'm not going to attack you, but feel perfectly free to attack me."

She didn't know where his sudden show of assertiveness was coming from, but she wished he'd cut it out. "I want you to go join Chance and Michelle."

"I prefer it in here."

"That's an order, John Doe."

"Come on, Sandy."

"I mean it!"

"Take it easy, Sandy."

"I'm going down for a swim."

"A cold shower would do just as well."

"Or another man. Maybe I can find a male flight attendant down by the pool."

"Good luck," he said, sounding very pleased with himself.

Damn it, he knew she was attracted to him. He not only knew it, he was trying to take advantage of it.

"Where's Sandy?" asked Chance.

"She went down for a swim."

"Don't you swim?" asked Michelle.

"I'm not in the mood," he said. "Incidentally, Chance, our dinner is all over the floor in there. I think the carpet's going to have to be cleaned."

Michelle nodded her head in understanding. "You had your first fight, huh? Don't worry, it will be all the more fun to make up later."

"You two had a fight?" asked Chance, grinning.

"Not exactly," said Johnny.

"And the dinner ended up on the floor? Hey, I wish I had seen that."

"Some kid down by the pool threw a volleyball up on the terrace, and the noise scared her. Somehow the table got tipped over." He couldn't help smiling at the memory.

Chance was nodding. "She reacted fast, huh?"

"Very fast."

"Yeah, that's Sandy."

Michelle said, "We're going dancing tonight. You guys want to come along?"

"We're not going dancing," said Chance. "We're staying home."

"Chance, we've been in the house all day."

"We've got music here. We can dance without having to go out."

"But you don't have anything to drink?"

"So go home and get some of those little bottles you stewardesses all have and bring them over."

Random felt stupid standing around like a third party and wandered out to the laundry room. He looked around for cleaning supplies but didn't find any. The people who owned the place must have a maid. The hell with it, he didn't know why he was so worried about the damn carpeting. Well, yes, he knew.

It was because it was going to bother Sandy. She'd be in there on her hands and knees scrubbing the carpet. And it was for sure Chance wouldn't lift a hand.

He shouldn't have given her a hard time. She was right; he was getting as bad as Madrigal. It wasn't easy, though, knowing Madrigal was doing with some woman he didn't even care about what he himself would like to be doing with Sandy. And he hadn't been lying—he did care about her. She was the kind of woman he'd been beginning to think he'd never meet, and then he'd had to meet her under these circumstances.

He would apologize when she got back. Being on good behavior for a few more days wasn't going to kill him. But letting his guard down and trying to get her to do the same thing just might.

And he wasn't one hundred percent convinced she wasn't the leak, anyway.

Chapter 8

Michelle had not only returned with miniature bottles of liquor, she had also brought candles that were now strategically placed around the vast living room. A slow and sexy song was coming out of the enormous speakers, and Michelle and Chance, their bodies wrapped around each other, were swaying to the music.

Sandy and Johnny looked in at them from the door to the hallway.

"It seems a shame to disturb them," said Johnny.

"It's past his bedtime."

"Let him finish one last dance."

Sandy didn't trust Chance. She was sure his next request was going to be for Michelle to sleep over. And if that happened, he would end up getting no sleep at all, and the burden of guarding Johnny would all be on her. No way—Chance was going to bed.

"Let's dance," said Johnny, his voice soft.

"I don't want—"

"Sure you do," he said, taking her hand and pulling her into the living room.

She started to protest, then, remembering they were supposed to be honeymooning, let him put his arms around her.

Her head reached midway up his chest, and she wasn't able to keep an eye on Chance and Michelle. Johnny was too tall to dance with; they must look ludicrous. He was bending down and resting his head on top of hers, and it made her feel like a child dancing with an adult.

The stirrings in her body induced by the contact of his body didn't feel childlike, however. She tried to move away from him a little, but his arms held her firmly. "Johnny," she complained, "give me a little room to breathe." Her heart wasn't really in the complaint, though.

"You're breathing. I can feel your breath on my chest."

"I can't *see* anything."

"You don't have to see, I'm leading. Just close your eyes and enjoy it."

He was wearing the black tank top she had bought in Coconut Grove, and it looked as sexy on as she'd thought it would. He didn't have Chance's body-builder physique, but he had something better—a smooth, tan chest that was strong without advertising the fact. It was also warm, and she could hear his heartbeat, which seemed a little fast to her, rather like her own. They weren't the right height for each other, though—they didn't fit together that well. Ideally, she should be able to place her head on his shoulder so that she could turn her face for a kiss. Maybe she *was* a midget. Maybe she should be looking around for another small person. Maybe she should stop thinking about fitting and kissing and start remembering who he was and what she was there to do, which had nothing to do with dancing.

She felt his lips move across the top of her head, and she shivered. My God, was the scalp an erogenous zone? She'd never heard that it was, but it was sure reacting like one.

He moved one arm down, and the next thing she knew his hand was snaking up between their bodies and then cupping her left breast. "Cut it out," she warned him.

"And that was my best move in high school."

"We're not in high school, Johnny."

The wayward hand was removed but next it traveled down to cup her rear end. She let it remain there for a pleasurable moment before saying, "Please remove it. Was that another of your high school moves?"

"I have a lot of them. You want to see?"

"You must have had quite a reputation."

"Not as good as I wanted it to be."

The next thing that happened was that his hands went to her waist and she was suddenly lifted so that they were on eye level. "Put me down," she demanded, made to feel like a child again. Instead of dropping her, he let her slowly slide down the length of his body, and the sensation was similar to riding a roller coaster. This time she felt like ordering him to do it again, but she desisted.

Great. Now she was all worked up and she'd never get to sleep.

"God, you guys look so cute together," said Michelle, and Sandy pulled back to get a look at her. She looked rather bleary-eyed, and so, she noticed, did her partner.

"Have you been drinking?" she asked him.

"Hey, how about dancing with me?" asked Chance, letting go of Michelle and holding out his arms to her.

"I'm not into incest," said Sandy.

Chance gave her a big smile. "It was me who taught you to dance, remember?"

"Give it a rest, Chance."

Chance put on his "Aren't I endearing?" smile. "Hey, Michelle, isn't my little sister cute when she's mad? I spent hours teaching her to dance, and now she won't even dance with me."

Giving him a murderous look, Sandy moved into Chance's arms and saw Michelle grabbing Johnny. She had a sudden horrible thought that maybe Johnny would go for Michelle's charms the way Chance had.

"This hasn't turned out to be such a bad assignment," whispered Chance, nearly asphyxiating her as he breathed alcoholic fumes into her face.

"God, Chance, you reek. You've been drinking, haven't you?"

"Not me, McGee."

"That was a rhetorical question, Madrigal. I can tell by your breath you've been drinking. And your eyes. And the way you're stepping all over my feet."

"So I had a few, big deal. I'll exercise it off."

"You'll *sleep* it off. It's eleven, Chance. I think it's time you sent your girlfriend home."

"It looks to me like I'm not the only one having a love life around here."

"What's that supposed to mean?"

"Just that you and Johnny seem to have gotten pretty cozy."

"Thanks to you. Thanks to having to pretend we're on our honeymoon."

"I think not, McGee. You've never followed one of my suggestions before. I never would've thought you were the type to go for a bent cop."

"I'm not the type," insisted Sandy.

"Hey, admit it, you're only human."

"I am not," she protested, then realized what she had said. "Of course I'm human, but I'm not depraved."

"If you want my opinion, McGee, Johnny isn't depraved, either. I like him."

"Well, good. Why don't *you* dance with him?"

Chance pulled her closer and started to feel her up.

Sandy thrust him away from her, just about annoyed enough to throw him across the room. Only deference to the lieutenant's brother-in-law's expensive furniture prevented her.

"Go to bed, Madrigal," she ordered him in a low voice. "I don't want you useless to me tomorrow."

"I'll go to bed," he said to her, "but not alone. Michelle's spending the night."

"Like hell!"

"Hey, what's the problem? You jealous that I'm getting some and you're not? I'm sure Johnny would be willing. Hey, Johnny—'' he started to call out over the noise of the music.

Sandy shoved him back against the wall. ''Either you go to bed now, Madrigal, or I'm calling the lieutenant and requesting he replace you.''

''Let me talk to him before you hang up. I want to warn him of a little conflict of interest we might have here with you and Johnny getting close.''

''You son-of-a—''

''Don't say it, McGee. Let's try to keep it nice and friendly here. We're still going to have to live together after tonight's over.''

''Is there a problem?'' asked Johnny, suddenly beside her.

''Where's Michelle?'' she asked.

''Went to the bathroom.''

''He's drunk,'' said Sandy. ''Why don't you make him some coffee?''

Sandy went down the hall and saw that one of the bathroom doors was closed. She knocked.

''Come on in,'' Michelle called out.

Sandy hoped she wasn't expecting Chance. She opened the door and saw Michelle doing some repair work with an eyeliner pencil.

''This has been fun, hasn't it?'' asked Michelle.

''Loads of fun,'' said Sandy.

''It was Chance's idea to stay home. I would just as soon have gone out dancing and left you kids alone. The last thing you probably want is your brother around.''

''I'm sorry to have to tell you this,'' said Sandy, ''but I think you better leave. Chance's wife is expected back in the morning, and she's always early.''

"Wife?" asked Michelle, but she didn't look doubtful.

Sandy nodded. "Sorry."

Michelle shrugged philosophically. "I should've known it—all the good ones are married."

Sandy stayed in the bathroom for a few minutes in order to avoid any fireworks that might ensue. When she got back to the living room, Chance was seated on the couch, his arms folded across his chest, fury in his eyes, and Johnny was seated on the other, a diffident look on his face. He didn't look as though he wanted to take sides in this.

"You want anything before you go to bed?" she asked Chance, hearing—and hating—the motherly tone of her voice.

"You've done me enough favors for the night," he said, his voice cutting.

"You had your fun, Chance. We're supposed to be working."

"You didn't have to lie and say I was married."

"What was I supposed to tell her, the truth? I could've been really rotten and told her you had a social disease."

"Well, thanks, partner—I owe you one."

"If you feel like staying up, Madrigal, I'd be glad to take the early shift tonight. I'm beat."

Chance got to his feet and then stumbled against the coffee table. "Forget it," he said, making his way slowly out of the room.

"You feel like playing some chess?" asked Johnny.

"No, I feel like getting into the hot tub. I feel sore all over from diving onto the floor."

He stood up. "Okay, let's go."

"I beg your pardon?"

"Well, you can't guard me with you in there and me out here."

"I could try."

Johnny was shaking his head. "I don't know, Sandy, I just wouldn't feel safe."

"You think I'd feel safe in a hot tub with you?"

"Who said I was getting in? I'll sit on the floor with my back turned the whole time."

"Right."

"You don't believe me?"

"No."

"You don't trust me?"

"Not as far as I can throw you, and that's pretty far."

He grinned. "What makes you think *I* trust *you*?"

"You should," she said. "I'm honest."

His grin faded. "Maybe if you knew the circumstances—"

"You going to tell them to me?"

"I can't."

"They wouldn't make a difference anyway."

His look was enigmatic as he got up off the couch and headed for the hall. "I'm turning in," he said, not waiting for her to reply.

Sandy suddenly felt exhausted and didn't know whether she'd be able to hold out until four. She would have given anything to be able to curl up in bed with a book and read until she fell asleep. Preferably something nonfiction, something with a title like "How Not to Fall in Love With the Wrong Man." She could use a book like that. She could use any advice she could get.

She had to talk to someone, and she didn't see any harm in calling Annie. There was a white phone, made to look like an antique, on the end table. She picked it up and was astonished to hear Chance's voice. She would have bet he'd pass out as soon as he got to bed.

"She lied to you," he was saying, his voice soft and sexy.

"Why would your sister lie to me?" she heard Michelle ask.

"She's a practical joker," said Chance. "She's always doing this to me. You should hear about some of the jokes she played on me in high school."

"I'm sorry, Chance, but I don't think your sister was lying."

"She's an idiot."

"She's no such thing. She couldn't have been nicer to me."

"I swear to God, Michelle, I'm not married."

"That's what they all say."

"All?"

"You wouldn't believe how many married men hit on female flight attendants."

"I'd believe it."

"I thought you were different, Chance."

"Do me one favor, will you, Michelle? Come on by tomorrow and see if my fictional wife really showed up. Will you do that?"

"I'm flying to Dallas–Fort Worth tomorrow."

"When you get back then, okay?"

"I don't know...."

"Come on, Michelle, would I ask you to do that if I had a wife?"

There was a pause, then, "All right, Chance, but if she's there, you're going to be embarrassed."

"I'm not going to be embarrassed because she isn't going to be here, and she isn't going to be here because she doesn't exist."

"We'll see."

"Hey, I thought we had something good going."

"So did I."

"Don't you want to use that hot tub again?" he asked, and at that point Sandy was diplomatic enough to hang up.

One phone call. It wouldn't hurt. One phone call and maybe he could turn things around.

Johnny sat up in bed and reached for the phone. He hesitated for a moment, then grabbed it and brought it to his ear.

He heard Sandy say, "Oh, Annie, I have to talk to someone."

"Sure, Sandy, what's up?" he heard, and was about to politely hang up when he heard Sandy say, "I'm in deep trouble, Annie. I think I'm falling for a crooked cop."

A smile crept over his face, and he kept listening.

"Crooked? Chance?"

"I'm not talking about Chance. I'm talking about the witness we're protecting."

"You're kidding! I figured maybe something would come of you and Chance being alone for a few days, but I never would've figured this."

"Chance gets more obnoxious the longer I know him."

"But he's so cute."

"He's an air-head, Annie, believe me. All he ever thinks about are his muscles and the next time he's going to have sex. And I'm not even sure he thinks. It's probably just instinct."

Get back to the crooked cop, Johnny silently urged her.

"So tell me about him."

"What's the use? He's crooked *and* a snitch. How can I possibly feel anything for someone like that?"

"So what is it you like about him?"

"I don't know. Maybe it's just that compared to Chance he's a human being."

"You wouldn't fall for a guy that easily, Sandy. In fact, you're rarely interested in one at all."

"He's intelligent, he has a sense of humor—"

"Wait a minute. I thought you said he was a cop."

"He is."

"Intelligent?"

"Thanks a lot, Annie. *I* happen to be a cop."

"You're an anomaly."

"Whatever that is."

"Is he sexy?"

He could hear Sandy's sigh. "Well, I guess that's the real problem."

"I take it that's a yes?"

"He's very sexy. I don't remember ever being turned on this much by a man."

Johnny slid down in the bed, a beatific smile on his face.

"Maybe you're just bored, Sandy."

"You could at least assume I have the intelligence to know sexual attraction from boredom."

"I've been attracted to men out of boredom."

"Yeah, you and those musicians you used to go for, but I'm not like that. And it's more than just sexual attraction, anyway."

"So what do you want me to say? You seem to have all the answers."

"I want you to tell me I'm out of my mind."

"You already know that."

"I want you to tell me what a rotten, loathsome, snake in the grass he is."

"He's a rotten, loathsome, snake in the grass."

"But he doesn't *seem* like it, Annie."

"How much longer are you going to be on this assignment?"

"A few more days."

"You're not planning on going to bed with him, are you?"

"Don't be ridiculous! Anyway, Chance is always around."

"So wait it out, Sandy. Once you aren't seeing him anymore, you'll probably get over him."

"Do you really think so?"

"A crooked cop who's singing? He'll no doubt be put in the witness protection program and you'll never see him again."

"Tell me I'm too good for him, Annie."

"You *are* too good for him."

"Tell me this is just a silly infatuation and I'll laugh about it later."

"I'm sure that's exactly what it is."

"Then how come I keep fantasizing about getting him into the hot tub?"

Random sat upright with a start.

"Hot tub? They must be putting up witnesses in style these days."

"You wouldn't believe the style."

"Well, enjoy it while it lasts. Incidentally, your animals are doing fine."

Sandy moaned. "I don't believe I could've forgotten about them. I should've asked about them right away."

"Don't worry, they're fine."

"Fidel's eating okay?"

"Jack took Fidel for a long walk, and they both loved it. Jackson, of course, usually hides when I'm there."

"Oh, Annie, it's so good being able to talk to someone."

"I wouldn't think being with two sexy men would be all that bad."

"But they're men. You can't really talk to them."

Johnny took exception to that remark. But then, that was what he got for listening in on other people's conversations. Not that he regretted it. She was feeling the same way he was, and that was all he needed to know. One day soon this would be all over. He didn't think he'd bother to make that phone call after all.

She looked up from her book and saw him standing in the doorway. The air-conditioning had been chilly, and she had changed into her robe. Now she saw that he was wearing his, too. He looked handsome in the dark blue robe that set off the smooth tan of his skin. His chest appeared in a V, and below the robe she saw his strong legs and bare feet. He looked half wild and half civilized, and she found the combination devastating.

She gathered her legs up under her and pulled her robe closer at the neck.

"Want some company?" he asked.

"No," she said and heard the fear in her voice.

He ignored her answer and walked over to the couch. She thought for a moment that he was going to sit down next to her, but then he seemed to change his mind and sat down on the other couch. He threw a pillow on the marble coffee table and then swung his legs on top of it. He looked powerful and yet at ease, and the chill air in the room began to make her shiver.

"What do you want?" she asked him.

His mouth, which looked hard in repose, softened. "What do I want?" he asked softly, and his eyes told her she knew the answer to that.

"What are you doing out here?"

"I couldn't sleep."

He reached one hand behind his neck, and then it appeared again, holding a leather thong. Thick, lustrous brown hair tumbled around his face and shoulders, and one errant piece fell across his forehead, and he lifted his hand to push it back. She could feel her hand tingling, her hand that wanted to reach out and push back his hair and get lost in the feel of it.

There was an unreality about the moment, as if time had stood still. She knew it was a vulnerable time for her, and she had to act with great care or she'd be lost.

"Have a drink," she said to him. "It'll relax you so you'll be able to sleep. There're probably plenty of those little bottles around."

"I don't want a drink," he said, and she found his voice mesmerizing. In a moment he would have her hypnotized and doing whatever he wanted. Or maybe it was what she wanted that was worrying her.

She got somewhat agitated and shifted her position on the couch, her robe falling open a little in the process. She frantically pulled it together, suddenly aware that she was naked beneath her robe—and so was he. Two pieces of navy blue terry cloth were all that kept them from being totally exposed to each other, totally open.

She could feel her skin begin to heat up. "Look," she said, trying to sound indifferent to what she was feeling, "I really want to read this book."

"You haven't turned a page in ten minutes," he said, his chest rising and falling beneath his robe.

She was very much aware that her own chest was mirroring his movement, but she couldn't seem to control it.

"You've been watching me?"

A smile slowly took over his hard mouth, making it soft and inviting. "Let's play a game, Sandy."

"I don't want to play a game."

"Let's play 'What if?'"

She hugged herself. "I especially don't want to play that game."

"What if we'd met under different circumstances? Would you go out with me?" His tone was mocking, but his eyes were dead serious.

"No."

"You didn't even have to think about it?"

"I don't date cops."

"Never?"

"Never."

"What if I weren't a cop?"

She had to put a stop to this game or end up losing it. "I'm afraid you're not my type, Johnny," she said, then waited for the anger she knew would come.

Instead, he looked about to laugh, and the warmth in his eyes astonished her. He was acting like a man who'd been told he was loved, not like one being rejected.

"Nothing personal," she added.

"If you'd asked me when we met, I would've said you weren't my type, either." There was no mistaking that he had since changed his mind.

"Johnny, I'm the only woman around. If Michelle were the one guarding you, you'd be attracted to her."

The look in his eyes was distracting. It was like the look a cat gets when it's watching a mouse, waiting for an opening in order to attack.

She felt compelled to talk. "It has something to do with being under my protection. Hostages are often attracted to their captors."

Now his eyes were openly mocking her. "That's a different situation entirely. I'm not afraid of you, and I'm not under your control. And I'm not attracted to you because you're protecting me. I'm attracted to you, Sandy, because I'm getting to know you and I like what I'm finding out."

It had become a contest of wills, and she knew she had to be the one to win. "You don't know me at all, Johnny."

"I know you. I know right now you're wishing I'd go back to bed because I'm forcing you to confront something you're afraid to face."

"Is this psychoanalysis time?"

"Now you're putting up that tough front of yours that you use as a defensive measure with men."

"Go to bed, Johnny." She was beginning to feel a little desperate.

"I'll bet you weren't like that before you became a cop."

Okay, she was going to have to fight dirty in order to win. "Why don't we analyze *you*, Johnny? What makes a nice boy from Indiana turn into a crooked cop?"

He leaned forward, and now there was no mistaking the look of passion in his eyes. "It's not going to work, Sandy. You're not going to get rid of me that way."

"Maybe you'd like to tell me the right way to do it?"

He was up from the couch and kneeling in front of her, his hair swaying from the sudden movement. She had an urge to trace his cheekbones with her fingers and smooth the lines at the corners of his eyes. She wanted to reach out and close his eyes so they wouldn't mesmerize her any longer, to feel his lips on hers.

He reached for her shoulders, and she felt his warm fingers tighten. A sudden, delicious spark ran across her shoulders and down her spine, her breasts catching fire. If only he knew she found him almost irresistible, that in a moment she would be ready to—no, she shouldn't even think of it.

His kiss when it came was wondrous, the heat magically consuming. She felt soft all over, vulnerable and exposed, and didn't even mind it. She had never felt so female before, and she cherished the feeling.

There was the sound of lips pulling apart, the sensation of hands being removed, and she felt the change in temperature as his body withdrew from her. She was being abandoned and was already grieving over the loss.

Only his eyes were touching her now, and there was a question in them that she couldn't answer. He got to his feet and headed for the hallway, and the sight of the navy blue robe stretched over his back as he left her brought tears to her eyes.

She sat as if in a trance long after he was gone from her sight. She couldn't think, couldn't concentrate. She was all tingling nerve ends and unfulfilled needs and massive confusion. It was like a dream, a frustrating dream that she couldn't quite awaken from. It was like waking up before the dream was over and not being ready to abandon it. So you did all the right things and tried to summon it back, but it was gone, lost, out of your control. It was the kind of dream that took a long time to fade and that you fought to hold on to, even though you knew it was a losing battle.

It was the kind of dream she never wanted to wake up from.

Chapter 9

Wake up, Madrigal." She shook his shoulder, and he suddenly made a loud burping noise that subsided into snores.

Sandy shook him harder. "It's four o'clock, get up. I can't keep my eyes open any longer. Come on, Chance, I'm really exhausted."

He reeked of booze, and she wondered how many of the small bottles he had consumed. It must have been quite a few, as he could generally hold his liquor.

"What's the problem?"

She turned around and saw Johnny standing in the doorway. His face was in shadow, and he was naked to the waist. His jeans were slung low over his hips, and his hair was once more pulled back off his face.

She quickly averted her eyes. "I can't get Chance awake and I'm dead tired."

He stepped into the room and walked over to the bed. He stood beside her, looking down at Chance, naked and covered only by a black satin sheet that molded the hips beneath. "I think he had a few too many."

"I should've paid more attention," said Sandy, frantic with the thought that she wasn't going to get any sleep. During the last hour it had been all she could do to keep her eyes open.

"It was probably when we were in the other room. Want me to throw some cold water on him?"

Sandy shook her head. "I don't think it would work. It might rouse him momentarily, but as soon as I went to bed he'd fall asleep again. I guess I'll have to stay up the rest of the night."

"Come on," said Johnny. "I'll talk to you and keep you awake."

She gave him a suspicious look.

"I mean it—only talk. I'm too beat for anything else. We can both nap in the morning when he's finally awake. He'll have a hangover to occupy him."

Johnny led the way out to the kitchen, where he put a pot of coffee on as she watched him with a wary eye from the doorway. A jolt of caffeine was just what she needed; being alone with Johnny in the middle of the night was definitely not.

Her mistake was carrying the cup of coffee to the living room and sitting down on the couch. Johnny sat beside her, and as soon as she felt the warmth of his body touching hers, she knew her defenses were not only down, they were practically nonexistent.

"I couldn't sleep very well anyway," said Johnny.

She ignored the remark, taking a sip of her coffee and hoping he wouldn't start anything.

"I had a lot to think about," he said.

"Conscience bothering you?" she asked in an effort to provoke him. Provoked, he might not be so nice—not so nice, and she might stop being attracted.

"Not at all. Why should my conscience be bothering me?" he asked. "I behaved like a perfect gentleman all evening and didn't take one drink."

"You're an absolute paragon, John Doe."

He started to chuckle.

"I wonder what your real name is."

"I don't suppose it would hurt to tell you that my real name actually is John. With one exception, I haven't been called Johnny, though, since the start of the first grade. My teacher called me Johnny and I quickly corrected her. My mother, however, persists in calling me that."

"You prefer John?"

"I thought I did, but I've rather liked being called Johnny by you and Chance. It sounds friendlier."

She thought of telling him that Chance made nicknames of everyone's name, but suddenly more talking seemed too much of an effort. She felt her eyes closing, and then sensed Johnny taking the cup of coffee out of her hand. "Take a little nap," he told her. "I'll keep watch."

She knew something was wrong about that, but she couldn't quite think what. And suddenly she was very comfortable, her head on something soft and with something warm wrapped around her shoulders.

She felt herself sinking into sleep.

* * *

He hated to disturb her, but there were noises coming from outside, and he thought he ought to check on them. She looked so peaceful curled up on the couch with her head in his lap. She looked as unselfconscious as a child, with one soft fist pressed up under her chin and her mouth slightly parted. She had changed her clothes and was now wearing a T-shirt and shorts, and he wondered whether the two of them in their robes had turned her on as much as it had him. She had seemed fragile in the robe, all swallowed up, and yet it was somehow easy to imagine the naked body beneath.

The sounds from outside increased in volume, and he shifted to ease her head off his lap. She opened her eyes. "What's wrong?"

"I don't know," he said, and was on the verge of telling her about the noises outside, but she had such a vulnerable look on her face, and her mouth was so soft and kissable, that he found himself leaning over to kiss it. Her arms went around his neck, and for a moment he forgot everything except the fact that kissing her was as sweet as anything he had ever known.

A pounding on the door brought them both upright. "Don't answer it," she said, instantly shifting gears and sounding like a cop.

"Something's happening out there, Sandy. I've been hearing noises."

She turned around on the couch and pulled apart the curtains. "There're people all over the place."

"It couldn't have anything to do with me," he said. "They wouldn't be likely to have anything to do with me," he said. "They wouldn't be likely to involve the entire building."

"You're probably right."

"On the other hand, we ought to find out what's happening. It could be a fire. It could be anything."

"They're not even dressed. They're all coming out of the apartments."

There was more banging on the door, and Sandy got up from the couch. Random beat her to the hall and headed for the door.

"No," she said, "I'm supposed to be protecting you, not the other way around."

That wasn't how he felt, though; he didn't want anything happening to her.

The pounding came again, and Sandy went past him and yelled through the door, "What's the matter?"

"There's a leak in the gas main and we're evacuating the building," someone yelled back at her.

"All right," she yelled back, then looked at Random. "It sounds too convenient to me," she said. "What do you think?"

"I'd say it's a little too much of a coincidence," he agreed.

"I'm going to check with the cop at the gate," she told him. "Go get Chance up if you have to dump ice water on him to do it. And make sure he has some pants on. And put some shoes on yourself."

"Yes, ma'am," he said.

She moved closer to him and looked up, then gave him a quick kiss on the cheek. "And thank you, Johnny."

"If that's for the kiss—"

"No, it's for everything."

He was dragging Chance bodily from the bed when she came into the room. "There *is* a leak in the gas main," she said. "All the buildings are being cleared out and we're supposed to go to the health club." She looked at Chance, who was now on the floor, half propped up against the side of the bed. He was naked and looked as inert as a dead body. "What do you think, is he able to walk?"

"I doubt it," said Random, grabbing Chance's pants and forcing them up over his legs. The hell with shoes; they weren't going to have to be running anywhere tonight. It was more important to get out quickly.

He reached under the pillow and found Chance's handgun and said, "You want him to have this or will you trust me with it?"

She paused only a second before saying, "You better take it. The condition he's in, Chance will end up shooting his own foot."

They managed to get the pants on Chance, and then Johnny stopped by his room to get a shirt to cover the gun he was carrying and a pair of shoes.

He was half carrying Chance when he met Sandy by the front door. She had put on running shoes and was carrying a straw handbag. She opened the door carefully and looked outside. Looking over her head he saw people in nightclothes hurrying to the stairs and then descending. At ground level, people were being hustled around the pool in the direction of the health club.

Sandy turned and glared up at Chance. "You better shape up fast, Madrigal. If there's trouble, we're going to need you." But Chance's eyes were glassy, and Johnny doubted whether he even comprehended what she said.

They went out, each with an arm supporting Chance. When they got to the outdoor stairs, Johnny hoisted him up and carried him over his shoulder. Chance didn't deserve to fall down a flight of concrete stairs just because he'd overindulged for once. Random wouldn't have minded overindulging himself tonight. Music, dancing, candlelight—hell, it was only normal. Except nothing was normal anymore.

Bunches of people led by men in gray maintenance uniforms were heading toward the health club. The three of them had started toward the pool when two maintenance men stopped them. "The health club's filled up," one of them said. "The rest of you are to go to the restaurant. There'll be hot coffee, compliments of Turnberry. Although why they think you need anything hot on a night like this, I'll never know." The guy was smiling, obviously making the best of the situation.

"Thanks," said Random, but Sandy had stopped dead on the pavement.

"Set him down and let him walk on his own," she told him.

He saw that she was half turned, pretending to help Chance down, and he wondered what she was up to. Then she drew her gun, and he turned in time to see that the two maintenance men had their own guns drawn.

He dropped Chance at the same moment she shot one of the men in the knee. The other man was momentarily distracted by the gunshot, and Random kicked the gun out of his hand, then tackled the man to the cement.

"What the hell—" the man started to say, but Sandy was already down on her knees and holding the gun to his head.

"How many more?" she asked him.

"Just us," the man said, listening to his friend's moans as he held his shattered knee.

"Kill him," she told Random. "He's lying."

He couldn't tell whether she was serious or not, but he didn't have to find out, because the man quickly decided to cooperate. He said, "Three more, but they're all outside the gate."

"Shoot him anyway," she told Johnny, getting to her feet.

He stood up and put his gun in his pocket. If she wanted the man shot in cold blood, she'd have to do it herself.

"Find something to tie him up with," she said, but at her words, the man scrambled to his feet, grabbed his gun and started to make a run for it. He turned around to get a shot off, and Sandy, sighting on him calmly, shot him in the chest. The man went down and didn't look like he'd get up again this time. She looked down at the man she had shot in the knee. "You want to make a run for it, too?"

When he didn't reply she reached into her straw bag and removed a pair of handcuffs. She handcuffed the man to the base of an umbrella table. It wouldn't stop him, but it would certainly slow him down. Particularly with all the blood he was losing.

"We're going to the health club," she told Random. "We'll be safe among all the people, and I can call the lieutenant from there."

"No," said Random.

"I'm giving the orders," said Sandy.

"No. No more," he told her. "No cops."

"We can't do this alone."

"No cops," he repeated. "The leak either has to be coming from the department or from one of you."

She gave him a stunned look. "You think if I was in on it I would have shot them?"

"I don't know," he said.

"You want to go back to my house? You can hang on to that gun if you think I'm out to kill you."

He shook his head. "I want to call the FBI," he told her, not knowing who to trust anymore. "It's their case, they can protect me."

"It couldn't be Chance," she said. "He wouldn't be stupid enough to get drunk if he knew what was going to go down."

"It should be obvious to you by this time, Sandy, that someone knows every move we make."

He saw the confusion on her face. Maybe it was guilt; maybe it was concern that her partner might be involved. "You trust the Feds?" she asked him.

"I've got to—I'm their witness."

"I don't like the Feds," she said matter-of-factly.

"Of course not. Cops never like the Feds. But I'm not going to stand around here debating the point with you. As the man said, there are three more outside the gate."

He dragged Chance out of the chaise where he had collapsed. "We're going to call the Feds. You can either go with us or stay behind, Sandy, it's up to you. In either case, thanks for saving my life.''

Chance had miraculously revived as soon as the agents arrived. His eyes were still bloodshot, and he wasn't all that steady on his feet, but she could tell he was making an effort. Not because of any desire to help her, though; he just didn't want to be brought up on departmental charges if it was found he was drunk on duty.

The Feds had driven them to an empty field, and five minutes later the helicopter had landed. As far as she could see, they hadn't been followed. And in a helicopter they weren't likely to be. Where they went now seemed to be out of her hands, but she and Chance were still supposed to guard Johnny. And that had been mostly Johnny's doing, which surprised her, since he didn't seem to trust either one of them. The Feds had been ready to take over completely, but he had told them of her fast thinking back by the pool. It hadn't been that fast at all, really. Something about one of the maintenance men hadn't seemed right to her, but it had taken her several moments to realize it was the bulge over his ankle. Chance would have caught it, too, if he hadn't been out of it.

One thing that had happened was that she was now wide awake. The danger had revived her as well as eight hours' sleep would have done.

The sun was just beginning to come up as she looked out the window. Down below was the Everglades, if she wasn't mistaken.

''Where're we going?'' she asked the agent who was seated beside the pilot.

"A remote cabin," he told her. "No one's going to find you there."

"In the Everglades?"

He nodded. "It's one of our safe houses, and we occasionally use it for hunting or fishing. There's no one within miles except for a Seminole who lives by himself and wrestles alligators. Just in case, though, we have an electric fence around the area, and five guard dogs are being flown in along with your supplies. They should be there shortly after we arrive."

"I like dogs," said Sandy.

"You won't like these. They'll be chained, and don't feed them no matter how much they howl. We want them good and hungry in case anyone tries to trespass."

"I'm not about to starve dogs to death," said Sandy, sounding incensed.

The agent looked amused. "You don't mind shooting a man, but you won't starve a dog?"

"That's right," she said. It made perfect sense to her.

"They're not going to be there long enough to starve. We'll be back the day after tomorrow to bring you out."

"That's not ten days," said Sandy.

"The trial's been moved up," she was told, and then the agent quit talking.

Damn! One of Rivera's men dead, one with his knee shattered, and he was going to be blamed for it. Not a bad ploy, either, evacuating the whole place and then herding them away from the others. They'd probably even done something to the gas main. He had to admit it was a classier operation than the bombing had been. Why the hell hadn't it worked? He knew one thing for sure, it was no thanks to him.

A gas main, though. Maybe they had planned to blow the whole complex, which would have meant hundreds of lives. Johnny's testimony must be dynamite.

He found that somewhere along the line he'd had a change of heart. Johnny had become his buddy; he enjoyed his company, and he had a soft spot for Sandy. One taste of the luxury of Turnberry, though, and he was hungry for the million dollars. He could picture himself buying an apartment there and then looking up those stewardesses. It didn't just have to be Michelle. He was sure he could have fun with all of them. Hell, the more the merrier, right? Yeah, it sounded pretty damn good to him.

He didn't have a choice, anyway. In the middle of the Everglades, he wasn't going to be able to get word out to Rivera. And after two foul-ups, he didn't trust Rivera not to take them all out the next time. He just didn't have a choice. He'd have to do it himself and make it look as though the leak was from the Feds, and that someone had gotten to Johnny and taken Sandy out at the same time. He could fake some injury to himself, just to make it look good. He was a cop; he knew how to arrange evidence.

Johnny didn't have much to look forward to anyway in the witness protection program, and Sandy— well, she'd die a hero's death. The department would probably have a big funeral for her, and he'd go and pay his respects. And right after that, citing grief over his partner's death as the reason, he would quietly quit the force and start living the life of a millionaire.

He'd do it tomorrow. He'd give it a little time, time for another leak and something to be set up, and then he'd do it. Maybe when they were sleeping. Better yet, he'd do it during the time when he usually slept, that way he could say they had knocked him out and then killed the others. He'd put Sandy's gun in her hand so that it would look like she got killed defending Johnny.

Yeah, and he wouldn't have to fake his grief for Sandy; he knew he'd really feel it.

Sandy could thank herself for her death. If she'd been friendlier to him, if they'd got something going, he might've cut her in on it. Nah, that was just trying to justify what he was doing. Sandy wouldn't have gone for it, not in a zillion years. She was so straight it was downright sickening. He didn't want to kill her, but at this point he had to in order to save his own skin. And from where he was sitting, Chance Madrigal was his number one priority. If he didn't look after himself, who the hell would?

And wouldn't he love to see the shake-up that would be going on in the FBI once this went down. Serve them right—he'd always hated the Feds. He and Rivera could have a few good laughs over that. He could picture them out on Rivera's yacht, maybe doing a little deep-sea fishing. They'd be having a drink, laughing about the chaos in the FBI; they'd be equals. Rivera would probably make him a partner. Hell, there was more he could do for Rivera than just pass on information. A former cop was valuable.

* * *

They circled before landing, and Sandy could see the glint of barbed wire circling the perimeter of a square acre of jungle with a burned-out area in the middle. Even from this distance it looked like it would be teeming with insects and alligators. This was the kind of place Bolivia would fall in love with; to Sandy, it looked like her worst nightmare.

They landed in a small clearing cut out of the jungle and fast becoming overgrown again. The sun had come up on a hot, overcast morning, and Sandy's clothes were sticking to her body as soon as she had jumped out of the helicopter and walked three feet. She could hear the buzz of insects all around her and wished she had been wearing long pants and a long-sleeved T-shirt when they'd left Turnberry, instead of the gym shorts and short-sleeved shirt, which was all she had now for the next two days. She didn't even have socks on, and her ankles were already beginning to itch.

She saw a small, dark shed and looked around for the cabin. "Your new home," said the FBI agent who had gotten out behind her.

"Where?"

"That's it," he said, walking ahead of her to the shed. He pushed open a door and motioned her inside.

"Are you telling me this is supposed to be habitable?"

"I've used it for fishing a couple of times. It's okay unless you get a heavy rain, and then it leaks all over the place."

"Where're the windows?"

"There aren't any. They'd let in too many insects, anyway."

She took a step inside, but it was too dark to see anything. The agent handed her a flashlight, and she turned it on. The room was about six by ten, and it was the *only* room. She saw a crate turned upside down to sit on, a folding cot and a couple of kerosene lanterns.

"I don't suppose it has a bathroom," she said.

"Sorry."

"How are we supposed to eat?"

"Food's being flown in. Mostly canned goods, of course, and bottled water."

"Didn't you ever camp out?" asked a cheerful-sounding Chance beside her.

"No."

"Well, now's your chance."

"Is this our only choice?" she asked the agent.

"Well, I've got a couple of other properties I could show you," he joked, then his voice became serious. "It's the safest place we could think of. No one could find you here."

"Hey, I don't see a TV," said Chance.

"Did you have television when you camped out?" she asked him.

"Hell, *I've* never camped out," said Chance.

No water, no electricity, no phone. And one cot for the three of them. It was beginning to be worse than her worst nightmare.

"Cheer up," said Chance. "I've got the utmost confidence that you'll have it looking like home in no time."

"I've got to take off," said the agent. "The other helicopter should be here within the hour. I'll see you again in two days."

At least he left her the flashlight. She went into the cabin and looked around. There was an army blanket folded up at the end of the cot. She felt it, found it wet, and took it out to dry in the sun. The only thing was, it didn't look as though there was going to be any sun. The sky was getting darker by the minute.

Johnny took the blanket from her and spread it over the mangroves. "I know this seems beyond the call of duty," he said to her.

"It does."

"But I have every confidence in you. You were great back at Turnberry."

"How are we going to shower?" she asked.

"By the looks of things, we're going to be able to shower in the rain."

Poor Chance, she thought. *No hot tub.* She turned around to tell him that and didn't see him. "Where's Chance?" she asked Johnny.

"He went inside. I wouldn't be surprised if he's napping on the cot."

She was about to protest that she was the one who hadn't gotten any sleep, but she realized she had no desire to nap on that cot in that dark cabin that was probably full of spiders and snakes.

She looked around but there was nothing. Nowhere to sit, nothing to do. She would gladly have cleaned the cabin, even painted it, if she'd had something to do it with.

"We'll make it," he said, and from the look in his eyes he meant more than just making it out of there or surviving for a couple of days.

She started to shake her head.

"We will, Sandy—I promise you." His eyes were as green and alive as the jungle.

"I don't see how you're in any position to make any promises."

"I might be in a better position than you think."

If that was supposed to elicit questions, she wasn't biting. She knew one thing for sure. No matter how she felt about him, she wasn't going to end up in the witness protection program with him. She'd have to love him a lot more than she thought she was capable of in order to give up her life for him.

That belief was shattered in the next moment, though, when he took her in his arms and held her close. A need that had been building in her rose to the surface, and her mouth lifted hungrily to his. And then it no longer mattered that there were mosquitoes buzzing around their faces or snakes somewhere in the grass or, for all she knew, alligators lurking behind the trees. She felt dizzy with the desire that was flooding through her, and she all but climbed his body in order to get closer to him.

She felt his legs give way, and then they both sank to their knees. They were closer to the same level this way and only a step away from being flat on the ground. Their hands went beneath each other's shirts, and moans escaped her mouth as warm fingers found her breasts. She arched her back, urging on his caresses, paying no heed at all to the sweat rolling off both of them.

At first she thought the noise was coming from inside her head. It didn't surprise her; nothing could really surprise her after the strong physical reaction he had so easily induced in her. When the noise grew louder, however, and combined with a strong wind that almost blew them over, Johnny's hands reluctantly removed themselves from beneath her shirt, and he finished the kiss soon after.

She saw him looking up and realized the helicopter had arrived.

They both stood, Johnny looking as shaken as she was feeling. He put an arm around her shoulder and pulled her close.

"I'm not going to apologize for that," he said.

"Oh, good."

He smiled at her and said something, but she didn't hear him this time, because the noise was now deafening as the helicopter hovered above them preparing to land.

The first man who got out wore a face mask and black gloves that reached past his elbows. He was a strange sight, but then Johnny said, "Dog handler" and she remembered about the guard dogs.

Five black Doberman pinschers were dragged out, thick chains around their necks. "They seem docile enough," said Sandy.

"Probably still drugged," said Johnny.

She wanted to pet them, to feed them, to play with them. The poor things had probably never known a loving home.

The dog handler went about his business, chaining the dogs to sturdy trees several yards into the undergrowth while the pilot unloaded several cartons.

When the dogs were chained the handler came over to them, taking off his mask. His face was young and freckled, and his smile friendly.

"I'm going to leave a dart gun with you," he said to them, handing Johnny what looked like a target pistol. "In case of an emergency—like one of them getting loose—this will tranquilize him. They'll be coming out of it in about a half hour. Don't feel sorry for them if they start howling for food—they've hardly had time to work up a good appetite yet."

"Thought I ought to warn you," said the pilot. "There's a new tropical storm in the Caribbean, and it seems to be heading toward Miami."

"We're too far inland to worry about it," said Sandy.

"It's just that if we're not back in two days, it might be due to a hurricane, if it turns into one. We brought you a radio with batteries so you'll know how it develops."

"At least we have something useful to do," said Johnny, after the helicopter had lifted off. "We can unpack."

"Oh?" she said, looking up at him with a smile. "I'm sure we would have found something else to do if he had waited a little while."

"Don't tempt me," he said.

"Why not?"

"Because we ought to get some of this stuff out of the sun."

"That shouldn't take too long."

His smile was devastating.

The first carton contained tinned meat and cans of vegetables, fruit and milk. The second held bottled water. She found the radio in the third, today's *Miami Times*, three Miami Dolphins sweatshirts in extra large and a deck of cards.

She held up one of the sweatshirts for Johnny to see. "I hope this doesn't mean we're staying out here until winter."

"Think of it as a souvenir of your trip."

"Something to remember you by?" she asked him.

"I'll give you something better than that," he told her, sending shivers through her body.

There were hunting knives, tin plates and cups, bars of soap, towels and even four rolls of toilet paper. And instead of kerosene for the lanterns, they had sent two battery-operated Coleman lanterns.

"It's not Turnberry," she said, "but they seem to have thought of everything."

She was about to walk into Johnny's arms when Chance came out of the cabin, stretching. "Is that food over there?" he asked.

"It's food," said Sandy.

"So when's breakfast going to be ready?"

"It's ready now," she said. "All you have to do is grab one of those hunting knives and open yourself a can."

"I don't suppose there's coffee."

Sandy was saved from thinking of a properly sarcastic reply by the sudden blare of music from the radio Johnny had been fussing with.

"Turn it down," joked Chance. "You're going to disturb our neighbors."

"Our neighbors are chained to the trees," Sandy informed him.

Chance took a look at the dogs and whistled. "They look mean, but they don't seem to have much pep."

"Give them a little while for the tranquilizers to wear off."

"Hey, Sandy," said Chance. "Why don't you get a little shut-eye? You didn't sleep all night, did you?"

"I don't know if I want to sleep in there."

Johnny took one of the lanterns and went into the cabin. He returned in a minute saying, "I don't see anything alive in there. It's none too clean, but it could be worse."

It already was worse. Sandy had to relieve herself, and the idea of going into the jungle to do it scared her. It would be just her luck to be squatting when an alligator came out from behind the bushes.

Not knowing what else to do, though, she grabbed one of the rolls of toilet paper and headed into the jungle. "If I'm not back in five minutes," she said, "send in the Marines."

"Hey, *I* was a Marine," said Chance.

Somehow, she wasn't surprised.

Chapter 10

Sandy wasn't happy with her new abode.

She had used branches to sweep it out, but the branches had left small green worms in their wake, and the worms clung to the rough floor and refused to be removed.

She had taken the cot out to air, but heavy thunderstorms after lunch insured that it would be winter before the blanket or cot would be dry again. The same could be said for their clothes.

Going to the bathroom outdoors the first time had been bad enough. Going a second time—to the same place—was to find it now overrun with insects that had been attracted by the smell.

The radio had bad reception, but it was good enough to relay the news that the tropical storm had now turned into Hurricane Boris and was heading in the direction of the South Florida coast.

Sandy had been saving the newspaper as a treat, but the rain had turned it into pulp before she had a chance to read it.

The rain revived the Dobermans, and they took up choral barking in a big way. Worse than the barks, however, were the occasional howls.

Lunch was canned chili and canned green beans.

After lunch they lit two lanterns and were playing poker, sitting cross-legged on the floor of the cabin. It was so hot and humid inside that Sandy's straight hair was beginning to curl. The open door was bringing in rain and insects attracted by the light, and her bare arms were providing a feeding ground.

"This is no Turnberry," she said, and the guys laughed.

"You ought to get some sleep," said Johnny.

"Afraid I'm going to win again?"

"No, I'm afraid you're going to fall asleep over the cards."

"I'm too tired to sleep." And she was. She had moved past exhaustion and was now in a state where she felt wired. Part of it she attributed to Johnny sitting next to her. He was so close, but there seemed little chance that they would get another private moment together.

Chance looked around the cabin. What a dump! He'd be doing them a favor if he killed them now. That way they'd all be put out of their misery, and he could get on with his life—in civilization.

How in hell were they even going to have sleeping shifts when they were all in one lousy room? He wasn't going to be able to make a plan. He was going to have to wait for his chance and move in for the kill. Sandy was going to be the problem. She always had her damn piece on her, and she was faster with it than he was. Well, she was going to have to make trips to the bushes—they all would. Frequently, by the looks of that canned food. He could ambush her in the bushes . . . nah, he'd let her die with dignity. She was a good kid; she deserved it.

He couldn't use his handgun. Ballistics would put two and two together and come up with his name. There were the hunting knives, but he had never cut anybody. Maybe in a fight he could use one, but otherwise, no, he didn't think he could do it.

It was so damn hot. You would think the rain would cool things off, but it didn't. His clothes felt cold and clammy, but his skin felt like he was being roasted over a barbecue.

Sandy didn't look so great, either. Her eyes were getting glassy from lack of sleep, and her skin looked awfully pale. Maybe when it came time for him to make his move she'd be too tired to reach for her gun. He wouldn't count on it, though.

Johnny looked okay, but hell, Johnny had been getting plenty of sleep. He was a good guy, the kind of guy he wouldn't mind having as a partner. Well, if Johnny had been smarter he wouldn't have gotten himself into this mess.

And if the rain didn't stop soon they were all going to start climbing the walls.

* * *

"Hurricane Boris," said Sandy. "They make it sound like the Russians are coming."

"I wouldn't want to be in Miami Beach right now," said Johnny.

Sandy said, "I'm not crazy about being here at the moment, either."

"It won't come this far in," said Johnny.

"You never know."

"Shut up and play poker, you two," said Chance. "I just raised, in case you hadn't noticed."

"Aren't *we* in a snit," said Sandy.

"Are you in or are you out?"

"Relax, Madrigal, it's only a game."

Chance got up and threw his cards on the floor. "I'll be back," he said, walking out into the rain.

"Talk about bad moods..." said Sandy.

"He misses the comforts of Turnberry."

"Don't we all."

"I miss being alone with you."

Sandy grinned at him. "We're alone now," she said, leaning over toward him.

He reached over and pushed her damp hair off her forehead. "On days like this, don't you wish you'd never joined the force?"

She took his hand and held it between her own. "It could be worse," she said.

"Tell me how?"

"We could be sitting here with *no* roof over our heads, and I could be alone with Chance."

"I want to make love to you, Sandy."

"Don't talk about it."

"It's all I can think about."

"I know, but don't talk about it. We're never going to be alone here, so there's no use talking about it."

Chance came through the door, limping a little. She figured he must have tripped over one of the vines. As Chance sat back down, Johnny got up and headed for the door. "Deal me out of the next hand," he said.

"We'll wait for you," said Sandy.

Chance had a mean look on his face. Something seemed to be eating him, and she wondered if he was still mad about her telling Michelle he was married.

"I hope you know what you're doing," said Chance, sounding surly. He might be a pain in the butt, but she'd never heard him sound surly before.

"What's that supposed to mean?" she asked him, sounding just as surly.

"Have you thought about what your future would be with a bad cop?"

"I don't see a future."

"That's good, 'cause there isn't one."

"Nice of you to be so concerned about me, Madrigal."

"I hate seeing you fall apart, that's all."

"I'm not falling apart."

"How could you even fall for someone like that?"

"Don't you think I'm asking myself the same thing? You like him, too, though—admit it."

"Yeah, but I'm not falling in love with the guy. I just never expected it of you."

"You think *I* expected it?"

"Yeah, well, you won't be seeing much more of him. You ought to try to get some sleep. You look half-dead."

"I feel like I'm on speed."

"You look like you're on speed," said Johnny, walking into the cabin. "Go on, try to get some rest. We'll keep quiet in here."

"Yeah, go on," said Chance. "You might not get the opportunity later."

Sandy gave in and went over to the cot. It hadn't looked comfortable, but it felt better than the floor, and it wasn't as damp. She lay on her back and closed her eyes.

How *could* she fall for someone like that? She would never be able to explain him to her family or friends. No one was going to understand her falling for a bad cop. She didn't understand it, so how could they?

If she married him she'd have to live under a false name for the rest of her life. She wouldn't be able to have any contact with her family or her friends. And did she really want her children to have a bad cop as a father? It would be worse to have children than not have them, and she'd always wanted children.

It was just a physical attraction; it had to be. What he had done went against everything she believed to be right. If he betrayed his friends, there was nothing to say he wouldn't betray her. Look at him, suspicious of her and Chance just because *he* couldn't be trusted.

It was just physical attraction; that was all. Physical attraction fueled by danger and by being shut up together for so long. As soon as this was over she would forget all about him and wonder how she could ever have been so stupid.

A drop of water bounced off her forehead, and she opened her eyes. As she looked at the ceiling, another drop came down and then another. She got up and moved the cot over a little. "It's leaking over here," she said.

"It's leaking over here, too," said Chance.

She looked around the room and saw minigeysers spouting up quickly all over the floor. She could also hear the howl of the wind as it blew around the cabin, and, just starting up, the howling of the dogs.

Why did they have to bring dogs? It was worse than cruel to have those dogs chained up in the storm. And why did animals have to be trained to be killers just because people liked to kill?

"We've got to feed them," said Sandy. "They're going to go crazy out there."

"We're not supposed to feed them," said Johnny, but he sounded uneasy about it.

"I don't think I can stand listening to them howl," said Sandy. "In a minute I'm going to start howling along with them."

"Hell, go ahead and give them the food," said Chance. "I could live without ever eating another can of that crap."

"I could just give them the meat," said Sandy. "It won't hurt us to be vegetarians for a couple of days." She looked at Johnny, but he didn't seem to approve. "They sent along more food than we need anyhow." Unless they were stuck there because of the hurricane, but it wouldn't hurt any of them to go on a diet.

"Just don't ask me to help you," said Chance. "I'm not getting near them."

Sandy got up and went over to the carton of food and looked inside. They wouldn't miss five cans of meat, and maybe it would calm the dogs down. No one was going to attack them out here in the middle of a hurricane, even if they had found out where they were.

She punctured the tops of the cans with a knife, then cut them off. Neither of the men got up to help her. Well, okay, so she was the only animal lover. Then why had Johnny been so nice to her pets? Maybe he'd just been trying to score points with her; maybe she didn't know him at all.

She put the five cans in the bottom of her straw bag and headed outside.

"Don't get near them, Sandy," Johnny called after her.

"Don't worry."

The wind was blowing so hard the rain was coming at her sideways. She was instantly soaked, and she thought how good it would feel when the sun came out again and they could all dry off.

The first four dogs lunged at her when she approached them, straining at the chains, their teeth bared. She kept her distance with each, throwing them the cans and watching as they practically devoured the tin along with the meat. At least it stopped them from howling.

The fifth dog was down on his stomach, his nose beneath one of his paws. He didn't look well at all. "Good boy," she said, keeping beyond the range of his chain. She heard him whimper but he didn't even lift his head.

Maybe he was trying to fool her. Maybe when she got close he'd ambush her. Except animals didn't think like that, and this one really looked sick.

"Good boy, what a pretty boy," she said, keeping her voice low and soothing. She took a few tentative steps in his direction, and he lifted his head now and fixed brown eyes on her. She paused for a minute in order for him to get a fix on her smell.

"You hungry, boy?" she asked, taking out the last can and holding it out. His head went back down between his paws.

She didn't know what she was being so cautious about; she had her gun. She could always shoot him if he attacked her, even though she wouldn't want to.

She carefully took a few more steps forward, watching him for any signs of attack. When she was in touching distance she set down the can. The dog whimpered again but didn't move.

Sandy moved in closer and squatted down next to the dog. She kept her left hand on the butt of the gun and reached out with her right to pet the dog. "You're not a bad dog, are you? You're a sweetheart."

She reached back for the can and found a stick that she used to scrape out the contents in front of the dog. He sniffed at it halfheartedly.

"Okay, so it's only chili and beans. Not exactly dog chow, I know, but it's all I've got."

The dog moved forward a little on his stomach, and she was thrilled when she saw his tongue reach out for the food. One thing she knew was not to mess around with an animal while he was eating, so she moved back a few feet to watch.

The foliage was so thick here that the rain had trouble penetrating. Still, there wasn't anything that wasn't wet, and she was actually dripping.

When she got back to the cabin she found the roof leaking in so many places that the word "roof" no longer had any meaning. She took one of the sweatshirts out of the carton. It was wet, but not thoroughly soaked, so she put it on.

"Were the doggies happy to see you?" asked Chance.

"One of them was. I think he's sick. He didn't even get up, and I went right up to him."

"There's always a coward in the crowd," said Chance.

Chance was lengthwise on the cot, and Johnny was trying, unsuccessfully, to staunch some of the leaks with leaves. Now leaves were raining down on them as well as water. He finally gave it up as a lost cause.

"Do you believe this?" asked Chance. "I think I'd rather take my chances on Turnberry."

"A hot tub would feel good about now," said Johnny, giving Sandy an enigmatic look.

"So would Michelle," said Chance.

"I'd settle for a waterproof poncho," said Sandy.

"I mean it," said Chance. "Why don't we get the hell out of here and take a taxi back to Turnberry? They wouldn't figure we'd return to the same place."

"Does anyone know how to get out of here?" asked Johnny. When there was silence, he nodded. "We're stuck, then."

"Hey," said Chance, "the radio's getting wet." He got off the couch and picked it up. He turned it on and nothing came out. He started to shake it, and then, without warning, threw it against the wall, where it shattered, the pieces falling to the floor and joining the puddles and the leaves.

Sandy was furious. "What the hell did you do that for, Madrigal?"

"The damn thing wasn't working!"

"You stupid idiot! All you had to do was give the batteries time to dry out."

"Dry out?" shouted Chance, sounding out of control. "How the hell are they going to dry out in here, will you tell me that? Where? Just show me one spot in this room that's dry."

"Now we won't even know what's happening," yelled Sandy, knowing she was losing it and not being able to do anything about it.

"All right, calm down," said Johnny, but they ignored him.

"Go on, find one dry spot!" screamed Chance.

"You act like a spoiled brat, you know that, Madrigal?" said Sandy.

Johnny figured they were going to end up killing each other at this rate. Chance was losing control, and Sandy was exacerbating things by arguing with him.

Maybe they should try to get out, but for all he knew they were miles away from anything. Booze would help; at least it would relax Chance. Hell, anything would help at this point. A hurricane was the last thing they needed. A hurricane meant torrential rains and winds, which meant they could be stuck here indefinitely with a bunch of dogs whose howling was going to send them all over the edge. From the sound of it, feeding them hadn't helped.

"Hell," groaned Chance, "a *tent* would've been better than this. They call this a *cabin*? A pup tent would have given us more protection."

Johnny saw that the floor was already covered with a half inch of water. The whole area could be ready to flood.

"Maybe we ought to start building an ark," said Sandy, and he saw she was trying to lighten things.

"We ought to build *some*thing," said Chance.

"What do the Seminoles live in?" asked Sandy.

Chance momentarily lost his scowl. "Condos in Fort Lauderdale."

"They must know how to use natural materials," said Sandy. "They didn't always own condos."

Chance grinned at her. "You know what they do, McGee? They wrestle alligators to their death, skin 'em, then use the hides to waterproof their roofs. You feel like wrestling some alligators?"

Sandy said, "At the rate it's raining, we'll probably have to. I expect to see one floating in here any moment now."

Chance sat down on the cot and stretched out his legs. "You know how wet I am? My damn pants are shrinking on me. You mind if I remove my pants, McGee?"

"Yeah, I mind," said Sandy. "You're not wearing anything underneath them."

"How would you know?" asked Chance.

"'Cause we had to get them on for you when you were passed out drunk."

Chance looked intrigued. "You saying you saw me with my pants off, McGee?"

"Believe me, Madrigal, it was no big deal."

Chance grinned. "Are you saying you saw me with my pants off and you didn't fall in love with me?"

"Don't flatter yourself, Madrigal," she said, and then they all started laughing.

Johnny was thinking it was a good thing that they could all enjoy the humor, but then he saw the expression on Sandy's face change.

"Hey, Chance," she said, "there's blood on your ankle."

"Probably leeches," said Chance.

Sandy paled. "No one told me there were leeches around here."

She went over to where Chance was sitting on the cot and knelt down to look at his ankle. In doing so she leaned against Chance's thigh, and he let out a scream.

"What's the matter?" yelled Sandy, jumping back.

Chance was moaning and holding on to his leg. "I think that cut on my leg broke open."

"Take off your pants," demanded Sandy.

"*Now* you say it," joked Chance, "when we're not alone." But Johnny could see he was really in pain.

Johnny grabbed a sweatshirt and took it over to Chance. "Stand up," he said to him, and when Chance did, he tied the sweatshirt around his waist. He reached underneath and started to unzip Chance's pants.

"Hey, I really don't think this is necessary," said Chance.

"Yes, it is," said Sandy. "I want to take a look at that wound."

"Is that all you want to take a look at?"

"That's all that's worth taking a look at," said Sandy, but now the pants were down and they could all see the open, festering wound and the way his thigh was swollen all around it.

Chance was beginning to look ill at the sight, and Johnny pushed him back down on the cot. They watched as Sandy fetched the first-aid kit. She started to apply antibiotic ointment to the wound but then stopped.

"This needs to be lanced," she said, her fingers gently pressing the swollen flesh around the wound.

Chance winced and shoved her hand away. "No one's cutting me."

"It's got to drain, Chance. Otherwise I think it could get really serious."

"You're just going to cut it without giving me whiskey or anything?"

She nodded. "I'm sorry."

She got one of the hunting knives, poured rubbing alcohol over the tip of it, and, holding Chance's hand tightly in one of hers, lanced the wound. Pus poured out, followed by clean blood. She wiped it off with peroxide, then applied ointment to the wound before taping it closed. It looked like a good job, but Johnny knew the weather was too humid for it to heal.

Sandy shook out a thermometer and shoved it under Chance's tongue. They were all silent until she removed it.

"Am I dying?" Chance asked her.

"You're running a fever. I want you to take a couple of aspirin."

"Oh, Lord," said Chance. "I'm going to get gangrene, and one of you is going to have to amputate my leg with a hunting knife."

"Not me," said Johnny.

"Shut up, Madrigal," said Sandy, "or I'll amputate your mouth." She looked at Johnny. "We have to rig something up to keep his leg dry."

"Put him under the cot. It's the only thing in here the water isn't going through."

"But the floor's flooding."

He watched as she picked up one of the plastic bottles that contained water. She dumped out the water and then used a hunting knife to cut it apart about an inch from the bottom. She ended up with a square piece of plastic that she taped over the wound.

"Maybe that'll help," she said.

"Thanks," muttered Chance.

She looked dead on her feet, and Johnny said, "You're not going to make it, Sandy, if you don't get some sleep soon."

She said, "I'm already feeling giddy. Do you think they're just going to leave us here in this?"

Johnny nodded. "There's no way they can fly in this storm. Hell, for all we know, Miami's being destroyed."

"I hope my animals are okay," she said. "Jackson gets frightened by thunder."

"They could bring a boat in," said Chance.

"Maybe they will," said Johnny.

Chance looked doubtful. "They probably think we're survivalists."

Sandy said, "You have to admit, Johnny, the Miami PD put you up a little better than the Feds."

"Maybe," said Johnny, "but I'd rather be wet than dead."

"There's wet and then there's wet," said Chance. "Do you guys remember the hot tub?"

"It was only yesterday," Sandy reminded him.

Chance's voice had a dreamy quality. "I was in this hot tub, surrounded by blondes—"

"He's beginning to sound delirious," said Sandy.

"I'm not delirious, I'm fantasizing. Don't you ever fantasize?"

Sandy said, "Right now I'm fantasizing a house on stilts with a tin roof. What're you fantasizing, Johnny?"

He gave her a look that shut her up.

"Yeah, Johnny, what're you fantasizing?" asked Chance, giving him an evil grin.

"Arizona," said Johnny. "The middle of the desert."

"You lie, man," said Chance.

Johnny said, "Some fantasies shouldn't be articulated.

"He should be in a hospital," said Sandy.

"It feels okay," said Chance. "You did a good job, partner."

"Does it hurt?" she asked him.

Chance shook his head. "Right now it feels numb."

"It shouldn't feel numb. It should be hurting you."

"Okay," said Chance, "it hurts a little. Does that make you happy?"

"Happy? *Happy?*" she asked. "You know what happiness is? A dry bed, that's what happiness is."

They both nodded in agreement.

The storm had made it so dark that she hardly noticed when the sun went down. She was huddled on the floor in an inch of water and eating cold, canned corn. She couldn't imagine more miserable circumstances. Chance was still feverish and going in and out of sleep on the cot. Johnny was sleeping sitting up, his face growing dark and unfamiliar with the growth of beard that was sprouting. She not only couldn't sleep, now her eyes felt wired open.

She had to get out of here. She *had* to. She didn't care if there were alligators out there; she'd take her chances. If she started walking and walked long enough, she had to come out of the Everglades at some point. She had to come to a road somewhere, or a house, or a store, or a gas station. Anything was better than staying here soaking wet, sleepless, miserable. Anything was better.

She got up and headed for the door. It wasn't raining much harder outside than it was in. It was dark out, but she'd take the flashlight.

She went over to the cot and leaned over Chance. She put a hand on his forehead and felt the heat. His leg was swelling up again, and they were almost out of antibiotic ointment. What he needed were a few shots of penicillin, and they didn't have any. He could die here, and there was nothing she could do about it.

She looked over at Johnny, whispered, "Good-bye," took up the flashlight and headed for the door.

"Where're you going?"

She looked back and saw Johnny watching her. "I thought you were asleep."

"Where are you going?"

"I have to get out of here." She stepped out of the door and headed across the clearing. She was almost to the mangroves when she felt a hand on her arm.

"You're not going anywhere," said Johnny.

"I have to. I can't stand it anymore."

"You'll get killed out there."

"I don't care," she said, trying to get out of his grasp. "I'd rather die out there than in the cabin."

"You're not going to die. Rain isn't going to kill us, Sandy."

"I can't sleep. If I don't get some sleep soon I might shoot myself."

"Come on back in, I'll put you to sleep."

"You can't. I don't know how to sleep anymore."

"Let me try, at least. If you can't get to sleep, then we'll all go."

"Chance is in no condition."

"I'll carry him."

"Let's just go now."

"Sandy, if we can get through the night, maybe in the morning the sun will come out. Maybe it will dry everything off and dry up Chance's wound and the dogs will stop howling and the Feds will come get us."

"Maybe not."

"Maybe not, but at least give it until morning."

She leaned against his chest, and he put his arms around her. "I need to sleep, Johnny."

"I know you do. Come inside and let me help you."

"I can't sleep anymore. I've forgotten how."

He picked her up and held her in his arms, her face pressed against his wet shirt. "Tell me about the desert, Johnny."

He was carrying her back into the cabin. "I'll tell you all about it."

He sat down on the floor, still holding her in his arms. She burrowed her face in close to him and felt his body warmth.

"Close your eyes," he said, and she felt fingers urging her eyelids closed. "Picture the sun," he said. "It's so bright you have to squint your eyes. So bright that everything in sight is dry. There's nothing green anywhere, and everything is dry. And you're warm. Warm and dry. So warm and dry that you can't keep your eyes open and you want to go to sleep. The sun is hot, and it relaxes you. You're so sleepy. So sleepy."

She wanted to tell him that she could feel it, feel the hot sun, but she was too sleepy to tell him, too sleepy to open her mouth. She was warm, and she was dry, and all there was was this gigantic sun turning everything yellow, everything white, and she felt warm and protected and too tired to think. Too tired to even think.

When he saw that she was asleep he closed his eyes. He would have given anything to be able to take her home. She belonged in that safe, cozy cottage of hers, with her cat and dog, her warm bed to comfort her, her roof to keep her dry, the things she had lovingly collected surrounding her. He found he identified her so closely with her house, that she seemed so alien to this environment, that he felt a deep shame that he was responsible for her being here. The protection of his arms was small comfort next to what she deserved. He wished now that he'd run from that cottage when he had the chance. His presence was doing her no good; his love was certainly doing her no good. But she had both, so long as she needed or wanted them.

He had to kill them. He had to kill them.

He woke up and stared at the ceiling, the wet, dripping ceiling. He felt nauseous and disoriented, chilled to the bone, and he knew he had to kill someone, but he couldn't remember why.

He started to roll onto his side, and the pain in his leg stopped him. It was a deep, throbbing pain that seemed to travel the length of his leg and numb his foot.

He propped himself on his elbows and looked around. Johnny was seated against the wall, his head forward, and on his lap was Sandy, asleep at last. He should kill them now while they were sleeping; he should put them out of their misery.

He saw his new black pants in a puddle on the floor. He couldn't kill anyone without his pants on. He had to get his pants, pull them up over his legs and stand on his own two feet. He tried to swing his legs over the side of the cot, but the pain was unbearable, and he collapsed onto his back. He had to kill them, but he couldn't remember why.

Where was his gun? He should have his gun on him, but he couldn't find it. How could he kill anyone without a gun? Someone had taken his gun away from him when he wasn't looking and shot him in the leg. Was he dying? Was he going to get out of here alive?

Rivera. Rivera wanted him to kill them. He was going to be rich, he was going to have a hot tub and all because of Rivera. He had to kill them first, and he had to have his pants.

Again he tried to swing his legs over the side of the cot, and this time he endured the pain. Slowly, carefully, he got to his feet. He found it was easier standing; when his leg wasn't bent it didn't hurt as much. He reached to the floor without bending his legs and picked up his pants. They were dripping wet, but he had to cover himself.

He saw the hunting knife under his cot and reached down again and came up with it. It was sharp, and he managed to cut the legs off the pants without much effort. They made raggedy shorts, but he would be covered.

He tried to put the pants on without bending his leg and almost succeeded, but the pain he felt from the fabric being rubbed over the wound was excruciating. He held back his cry of pain and tried walking on the leg. The foot was now tingling, so perhaps the numbness had been caused by it being asleep.

He paced back and forth over the flooded floor. Where was his gun? Where was his gun? God, he'd give anything for a drink right now. He'd trade his gun for a drink right now.

How could he kill them? Asleep, huddled on the floor in each other's arms, looking innocent and bedraggled and dear. How could he kill them?

He leaned against the wall and felt something hard hit his head. He looked up and saw his gun hanging from a nail. Someone must have put it there so that it wouldn't be sitting in water. It might be too wet to fire. He might not even get two shots off. He would say that someone broke into the cabin, found his gun, shot them to death and left him for dead on the cot. He couldn't move to save them because his leg wouldn't function.

They wouldn't shoot Sandy and leave him alive as a witness. He'd say he was outside taking a leak, that he had stumbled and fallen and couldn't get up. And then he'd heard the shots, but by the time he got back it was all over and the killer was gone.

He had to shoot them. He should do it now, because he might be too weak to do it later.

He took down the gun from the wall and held it in his hand. He had shot three men while on the force, and each time it was shoot or be shot. Maybe he should warn her, give her a chance to reach for her gun. But then he'd have to look her in the eyes, and he didn't think he could do that.

He lifted the gun and sighted on her. Why did he have to kill Sandy? Did he have to kill Sandy? Wasn't it just Johnny who had to die? He could wait for her to make one of her trips to the bushes, and then he could kill Johnny, throw his body into the mangroves, and tell Sandy that Johnny had made a run for it.

She wouldn't believe him. She was in love with Johnny; he could see it in her eyes. She was in love with a bent cop. She didn't know what she was doing, and he was saving her from a lifetime of regret.

His leg was stiffening on him. He tried to put his weight on his left leg and it no longer held him, and he went crashing to the floor, crying out in agony when the wound came into contact with the wet boards.

He must have blacked out for a moment, because when he came to Johnny was lifting him and carrying him back to the cot. He saw Sandy, propped up against the wall, still sleeping.

"You shouldn't have tried to get up," said Johnny, removing the wet bandage from his wound.

"I gotta get up," said Chance.

"No, you stay on the cot. Tomorrow you can get up, when the sun comes out."

"My gun. Where's my gun?"

Johnny reached down and picked up the gun from the floor and showed it to Chance. "I'll put it back up on the nail to dry it off."

"I wanted to cover myself. I didn't want to be naked."

"Good idea," said Johnny. "I think I'll cut my pants off like that."

"Is Sandy sleeping?"

"Finally."

"Good. That's good," said Chance.

"You want me to get you some more aspirin?"

"I'd rather have a drink."

Johnny smiled. "The least the Feds could've done was provide us with some booze."

"Damn right," said Chance.

Johnny handed him two aspirin and a bottle of water and watched while he took them. "How's the leg feeling?" he asked.

"It only hurts when I move," Chance told him, trying a grin but knowing it was coming out a grimace.

"Can I get you anything to eat?"

"You mean that garbage in the cans?"

"There's a can of peaches."

"Yeah?"

"I'll open it for you," said Johnny.

Chance ate the peaches with his fingers while Johnny put a clean bandage over his wound. The plastic cover that Sandy had made to keep his bandage clean was lost somewhere under an inch of water, but the roof wasn't leaking as much anymore, and the wind and rain seemed to be abating.

"You really think the sun will come out tomorrow?" Chance asked him.

"It's probably wishful thinking."

"Yeah. But it could happen, couldn't it?"

"Of course it could," said Johnny.

"And we could dry out."

"Well, it's still going to be humid."

"We could try to get out of here."

"That's what I was thinking," said Johnny. "You need medical care, and Sandy needs a bed, and I don't see why you two should have to suffer because of me."

"Listen, don't be so nice to us, Johnny."

"I care about you guys. You've been good to me."

"Don't be so nice to us, Johnny."

Johnny took the empty can out of his hand. "Get some sleep, Chance. Things will look better in the morning."

Chapter 11

Sandy woke to find her head on the only relatively dry spot in the cabin: Johnny's lap.

Her body felt miserable and aching, but her head was clear. Thanks to Johnny, she had gotten some sleep.

Something had awakened her, some sound, and now she heard it again, a creaking noise, loud and jarring. Johnny slept right through it, and Chance looked dead to the world.

She got up carefully and went over to take a look at Chance. She touched his forehead and found it too warm for him to be dead, as she'd feared for a moment. His wound looked no better, but it didn't look worse.

She heard the shrieking noise of an animal in pain and felt herself shudder. She went to the door and looked outside. The wind had died down, but the rain fell steadily. Many trees had been uprooted and some flattened to the ground by the wind. Some of the dogs could be lying crushed beneath them; some might have escaped. She heard the painful cry again and then, behind her, footsteps.

"I guess the sun didn't come out," said Johnny, coming up to her and putting his arm around her shoulders.

"Thank you for putting me to sleep."

"My pleasure," he said. "That sound, it must be one of the dogs."

"I'm going to go out to see."

"They'll be twice as dangerous wounded."

"Johnny, an animal is in agony. We don't need their protection anymore. I'm going to set them free."

"I'm going with you."

"No. They know me. I'm the one who brought them food. Anyway, I'm supposed to be protecting you."

"Take the tranquilizer gun with you," he said, and she realized she had forgotten about it.

"I don't know whether I could use it."

"It doesn't hurt them. It's just like taking a Valium: they can still function, but they feel mellow."

"You should have shot me with it last night so I could sleep."

"I doubt if it's strong enough to have any effect on a human. Although you don't weigh much."

"Don't start on me—"

"What did I say?"

"Never mind." She was sensitive about weighing less than a hundred pounds. Her friends never let her forget it, and her mother was always trying to fatten her up.

"Go on," he said, "take care of them. I'll open some cans for breakfast."

"I'll take them some more food. We *are* going to try to get out of here this morning, aren't we?"

He nodded. "I think it's a good idea. I don't like the look of Chance's leg. I think we should make a try while he can still walk."

Sandy found her straw bag, now shapeless from the wet but still usable. She took the handcuffs out of it, moved her gun to the waist of her shorts, then took the cans of meat as Johnny passed them to her and placed them in the bag. She'd carry the tranquilizing gun in her hand just in case.

She saw that Chance was awake on the cot and watching her. "How are you feeling?" she asked him.

"Not bad. I see you're feeling better."

"Sleep really helps."

"Where're you going?"

"To let the dogs loose. I think some of them could be trapped under downed trees."

"When she gets back," said Johnny, "we're going to try to find our way out of here."

"It's already decided, Chance," said Sandy, "so don't give us an argument."

"Who's giving you an argument? You think I like it here?"

"Be careful," said Johnny, walking her to the door. "If you need help, just give a shout. Or fire your gun."

"I'll be okay," she said, stepping out into the rain.

* * *

Chance swung his legs over the side of the cot to test the pain. It was still there, but no longer throbbing. It was more of a dull ache, along with a feeling of weakness.

"Rest it as long as you can," said Johnny.

"I need to take a trip to the bushes, if you get my meaning."

"Outside the door will do," said Johnny. "You need some help?"

"The day I need help with that . . ." said Chance, standing up and testing his strength. "But thanks all the same." He walked slowly to the door, favoring his left leg. It wasn't so bad; he could manage. He could get out on his own.

The time to make the move on Johnny was right now. But it might look strange if he went for his gun right now.

He grabbed the doorframe and stepped outside. Yeah, Sandy was nowhere in sight; no need for him to head for the undergrowth.

He had just unzipped his fly when he heard a screeching sound that hurt his ears, and then, directly after, a crash. Whatever it was sent shock waves through the hand that was holding the doorframe, and he turned his head in time to see the roof come crashing down on Johnny.

He stifled his natural impulse to go to his aid, thinking he had lucked out. Johnny had been taken out, and he hadn't had to lift a hand.

Not that the cave-in was likely to have killed him, but if it hadn't knocked him unconscious, then Johnny had a head of superhuman durability.

He finished his business, then zipped up his pants and moved back into the cabin. The roof had caved in in the middle. Half had buried Johnny, and the other half was just hanging there, ready to fall at the first little wind.

Chance pulled aside the rotted wood and saw Johnny crumpled on his side, one of the rafters across his head. He could be dead after all. He could be dead, and all his problems would be solved because he could swear to Rivera he had done it and prove to Sandy he hadn't. "I was just standing in the doorway minding my own business when I heard this crash behind me," he could hear himself saying to Sandy. She'd be crushed—hell, she loved the guy—but he would comfort her. And after a while she'd see that it was all for the best. Death was more heroic than disappearing into the witness protection program.

He had to make sure he was dead, though. He had reached out to move the rafter from across Johnny's head when he heard him moan. Not dead yet, then. Well, he could lift that rafter and then let if fall down; that should do the job.

There was another groan as he lifted the rafter, and he could see the blood coming out of Johnny's scalp. He was just about to let go of the rafter and let it do its job when Johnny opened his eyes and saw him.

"Sorry, buddy," said Chance, wishing he hadn't opened his eyes.

"What happened?" asked Johnny. "The roof cave in?"

"That's exactly what happened." Why did he have to open his mouth? How the hell was he supposed to kill a guy he was having a conversation with?

"Where's Sandy?"

"She's okay, still out with the dogs."

Johnny reached up and touched his scalp, and his hand came away covered with blood. Chance thought maybe he could just leave him there and let him bleed to death. He could tell Sandy he was already dead, and maybe Johnny's head wound would do the job for him.

Then Johnny made a mistake. He started to get up. Chance panicked, lifted his foot and kicked Johnny in the head. He slumped back down, his head bleeding more profusely. At the rate he was bleeding he wouldn't last long. Chance began to pile the rafters on top of Johnny's body, being careful to make it look as though they'd fallen that way.

One of the dogs lay dead, crushed by the tree. Two had gotten away, and by the looks of the holes in the ground, they were dragging trees behind them. Poor dogs. She wished she'd come out sooner.

The fourth dog lunged at her when he saw her, and she quickly stepped back out of reach. She aimed the tranquilizer gun, and he seemed to recognize it, because he began to bark, moving frantically in circles so that it was hard to sight at him. Her first shot missed, but the second got him in the haunch. The dog twisted himself around, trying to get at the dart and remove it, and then, almost magically, he began to calm down.

"Good dog," she said in a low voice. "Sit! Sit!"

With an almost bewildered look in his eyes, the dog sat, his tongue coming out of his mouth. "Good boy," she said, moving in closer to him. The only way she was going to get him unchained was to remove his collar.

She dumped out three of the cans of dog food onto the ground, out of his reach, and she saw him strain forward, but he was still sitting.

"Good boy," she said again, and walked right up to him. He let her pet his head and stroke his back while she wondered how long the effects of the tranquilizer would last.

He allowed her to take off his collar, and still he sat there, well trained and obedient.

"Eat, boy, eat your dinner," she said. He looked at her but didn't move.

She went back to him and bodily lifted him from his seated position, then led him over to the food. When she left him, he was devouring it in great gulps.

She had left the friendly dog for last, afraid to find him dead. She found him on the ground again, but looking better, and when he saw her he began to whimper.

She was so certain it wouldn't require the tranquilizer gun for her to get near him that she almost didn't use it. Then she thought of Johnny and Chance. Untranquilized dogs running loose might be a threat to them. She sighted on the dog and grimaced as she saw the dart hit him in the side. She waited a minute for it to take effect, then walked to him.

She stroked his head as she removed his collar, then dumped out the last two cans of food. The dog seemed to want attention more than food, and she spent a few minutes petting him and talking to him before leaving him to eat.

She wondered what would happen to the dogs. No matter what, they would have had a taste of freedom before they died or were captured. They might even survive.

She saw the collapsed roof as soon as she reached the clearing. Then she took in the sight of Chance, staggering around in front of the demolished building. It was only then that she realized Johnny was nowhere to be seen, and she broke into a run.

"What happened?" she yelled at Chance, dropping the tranquilizer gun, reaching instinctively to pick it back up, and then abandoning it.

She stopped and grabbed him by the shoulders. "What happened? Where's Johnny?" She knew when she saw the look in his eyes that something was terribly wrong.

"Oh, God, Sandy," he said, his voice agitated, "the roof collapsed on him."

"Where is he? Did you get him out?" She tried to move past him to where the doorframe and three of the walls still remained, but he held on to her shoulders, his grip steely.

"Don't go in there, Sandy." Chance's voice sounded suddenly hushed.

It was the sound of death, and she freaked out. "Let go of me. I have to go in there."

"No, Sandy, no." He was trying to put his arms around her, but she fought him off.

"He's alive in there, Chance, I know it. Let go of me!" she implored him, hating her size which was no use when pitted against Chance's muscles.

"Listen, Sandy, listen to me—he's dead."

"I want to see him."

"No. Believe me, you don't."

"You're lying to me! Johnny isn't dead." She was pounding him on the chest, her blows futile.

She tried to reason with him. "Just let me look, Chance, please let me in there. I just want a look at him, that's all."

"I don't want you going hysterical on me, Sandy."

"I'm not going to be hysterical unless you don't let me in there."

Shaking his head, an infinitely sad look in his eyes, he let go of her shoulders and stood aside.

Suddenly she was afraid to go in, afraid of what she'd see. If she didn't go in, would Johnny come walking out of there in a minute? If she went in, would that be admitting he was dead?

She stepped through the doorframe and paused. Rain poured steadily down on a pile of rubble at the back of the cabin, and she thought she could see…yes, she could see a stream of blood that was mixing with the rain and forming a river of pink.

Her hand went to cover her mouth, and she turned around, prepared to beg Chance to go in with her, and how she reacted so quickly she would never know, but there was Chance in the act of bringing the butt of his gun down on her head, and her leg seemed to move of its own volition, coming up and kicking him hard in his wound.

His scream was shattering as he was thrown on his back, sliding a few feet in the mud. He still had his gun in his hand, but hers was also out now and pointing at him. The bandage had come off his wound, which was open and bleeding. Betrayal was written in large letters across his face.

"Sandy, I was only—"

"Throw it over here, Chance."

"Will you let me explain?"

"Throw the gun down, Chance, and then you can try to explain."

Nothing needed explaining, though. Everything was suddenly very clear.

He moved to a sitting position in the mud, and both hands were now on his handgun, sighting on her head.

"Why are we holding guns on each other?" he asked, trying to grin at her boyishly, but the grin was macabre.

"I never would have believed it was you."

"I wasn't going to kill you. I was just going to knock you out."

"What's the point of lying, Chance? I knew the roof had already caved in. I would've called you a liar."

"I don't want to kill you, Sandy."

"You don't have much choice now, do you? But I'll get a shot off, too, Chance, and it won't be to kill. I'll shoot you in your bad leg and shatter all the bones, and you'll be left to die in your own rot. Slowly."

The barking startled both of them. Sandy looked up, and Chance looked around, as the Doberman came bounding into the clearing. He looked ferocious, but Sandy recognized him. Chance, though, scrambled to his feet and started to run. He stumbled and fell, and the dog went right by him and ended up at Sandy's feet.

She trained her gun on Chance's back. "Throw it behind you, Chance," she ordered him.

She saw him hesitate a moment, then get to his feet. He kept his back to her. "How long can you hold it on me, Sandy? Until help comes?"

She realized that she couldn't see what happened to Johnny and keep Chance in her sights at the same time. He was bigger than her, meaner, and would find some way to outsmart her. She wouldn't be able to hold a gun on him and at the same time handcuff him or tie him up. It was useless. She had to either shoot him or let him go, and she knew she wouldn't be able to shoot him.

"I'm going to walk out of here, Sandy," he said, taking a few steps across the clearing. "You can shoot me in the back if you want. Otherwise, I'm walking out of here."

She kept her gun pointed at him until he disappeared into the mangroves. He wouldn't get far with that leg the way it was. He'd never be able to hide from the police, the Feds and the criminals he worked for.

She slid her gun back in her waistband and rushed into the cabin. She listened for a moment, hoping to hear groans coming from the debris, but there was only the sound of rain coming down steadily.

Slowly and carefully she began to remove the rubble. She struggled with cross beams, wishing she had Chance's muscles, hoping she wasn't too late. She didn't believe he was dead; she couldn't believe it.

When the last bit of rubble left him exposed, she looked at the pale, bloody face and gasped. His eyes were open and he looked dead, but then she saw a shadowy green flicker and his mouth began to move, but no sound came out.

"Oh, Johnny!" she cried out, rushing to him and kneeling down. "Oh, Johnny, for a moment there—"

"I'm not dead yet," he said, his voice the merest whisper. "Where's Chance?"

"I had to let him go."

"I was afraid he'd kill you. I tried to yell out, to warn you, but a beam was across my throat and I couldn't make a sound."

"Let me try to find the first-aid kit," she said, getting up.

"I'm all right. Probably bruised, but nothing seems broken."

"But your head—"

"Not as bad as it looks, I'm sure. You know how head wounds bleed. I think we'd better get out of here. He might come back."

She helped him to his feet, and he seemed to be all right. She held two fingers up in front of him.

"Two," he said. "I probably have a concussion, but it's not that bad."

She put her arms around him, and he held her close. "I'm sorry about your partner," he said. "I know you cared about him."

"He was going to kill us."

"I don't think he wanted to."

"You're more forgiving than I am, Johnny. To do what he did—" She broke off, remembering that Johnny was a bad cop, too.

She cut the sleeve off her sweatshirt and tied it around his head in case he started bleeding again. The way they looked, the two of them were going to scare anyone they met up with.

Outside, the dog was waiting by the door. "I see you have a friend," said Johnny.

"He can come with us," she said. "At least he scares Chance."

Johnny patted the dog on the head, and the Doberman wiggled all over like a puppy. "This was one of our guard dogs?" he asked, disbelief in his tone.

"The other four were vicious. Four out of five isn't bad."

He was going to die in the jungle. He'd managed to get away from Sandy without getting shot, and now he was going to die in the damn jungle.

He was in so much pain from his leg that he would have been glad to tell a doctor to cut it off and be done with it. Be done with the pain that now seemed to be coming from every part of his body.

He stumbled through the jungle, grabbing on to trees and vines for support, seeing all around him the damage done by the hurricane. Once he heard barking in the distance, and he thought that was all he needed, some crazed, hungry Doberman attacking him and eating him for dinner. That was all he needed to make it a perfect day.

He thought about his mother and wondered why he had ever left home. She wouldn't let them do this to him. She would put him in bed and bring him food and wouldn't let anyone hurt him ever. She was the only person who had ever loved him unconditionally, and she'd probably die of a broken heart when she knew what he was in for.

He knew that there were people who would kill themselves at this point. People who would say to hell with life and end it. He knew he couldn't do it. As long as there was even the slightest chance he could get out of this, he couldn't do it.

Johnny had to be dead. All that blood, he couldn't have lived. He'd go to Rivera and tell him he'd taken care of the witness and to get him the hell away. He wouldn't even care if he wasn't paid the million. He'd take what he could get and offer to work for Rivera down in Colombia. An ex-cop had to be good for something.

And hell, miracles still happened; he could prove it by the fact that the sun had finally come out. After he'd thought it was never going to stop raining, not in his lifetime anyway, the sun came out and steam started to rise from the jungle floor and the mosquitoes appeared out of nowhere and began to swarm around him. Flies were thick on his wound, and as soon as he brushed them off, they were back again. And as if he hadn't lost enough blood, mosquito bites began to appear with regularity on his arms and legs and face.

Oh, yeah, jungles were great. Maybe he wouldn't volunteer for Colombia after all. Maybe Mexico, somewhere dry and barren.

He stepped off mud and found himself walking in three feet of water. It felt good on his leg, and he continued walking, hoping that he wasn't now in alligator territory. It was probably all alligator territory, though, and he had his gun with which to scare them off. The blood, though. They might be attracted by the blood. No, that was sharks; he wasn't sure if alligators went for the scent of blood.

At first he didn't believe it when he saw the wood house with the pier out in front and the air boat tied to the pier. Fearful that maybe he was feverish and hallucinating, he thought it was one of those mirages people often saw in the desert.

Then he heard the voices and the laughter and saw three young guys in cutoffs and baseball caps, carrying cans of beer, come out of the house and stand on the dock, and he knew he wasn't hallucinating because in his hallucination they would have been three young women.

"Hey!" he yelled, and saw the men turn in his direction.

"Hey!" he yelled again. "You guys got a phone?"

He walked right up to the dock, and one of them reached down a hand to help him. And then one of the others was handing him a beer, and the third was bringing out a folding chair, and Chance began to tell them the story of the armed and dangerous prisoner who had shot him and then taken off.

The Doberman seemed to be leading them through the Everglades. He would run ahead of them, then wait until they caught up, then take off again. Sandy didn't know how the FBI's dog could know his way around any better than she did, but they had no idea where they were going, and at least he tested out the terrain for them.

When the sun broke through the clouds, Sandy lifted her face to the sky. "I can't believe it," she said to Johnny.

"Maybe it'll turn out to be a good beach day," he said, and she knew he was trying to get a smile out of her.

A moment later they were fighting off swarms of mosquitoes and neither of them was smiling. As suddenly as they arrived, though, they apparently got enough to drink and moved on. Now she could hear birds in the trees and rustling noises all around, but at least she was beginning to dry off. She thought she could face an alligator if she was dry.

"If we get out of here—" began Johnny.

"We're going to get out of here."

"If we do—"

"I don't want to talk about it."

"This might be our last chance," said Johnny.

"Don't even say that word."

"What word?"

"*Chance.*"

He was silent for a moment, then, "He might have had his reasons."

"I'd expect that from you. I'm sure you had yours, too, didn't you, Johnny? Everyone who's ever gone crooked always has reasons. Just tell me what kind of reason would make you kill your partner? You don't have a reason for that, do you, so just shut up." She was hating herself, hating herself for the way she felt about him. Hating the way that just looking at his back, his tight rear end in his jeans, made her feel. Why couldn't he have turned out to be ugly and surly, the way bad cops were supposed to be? Why did he have to look like a damn hero?

"I think we should talk, Sandy." He sounded so reasonable that she wanted to boot him in the rear end and send him sprawling. Then she'd step right over him and walk out of his life, and maybe, just maybe, she'd be able to forget him.

"Save your strength, Johnny. We aren't out of here yet," she warned him.

"I'm not that tired, are you?"

"Let's just concentrate on making it out of here."

"I just want to say one thing, Sandy, and then I'll shut up. No matter where I end up, under what guise, what pseudonym, I will never forget—"

"Shut up!" she screamed at him.

"What did I say?"

"What is this, your final speech before the curtain comes down?"

"Nothing that dramatic."

"It sounded like it to me. I don't want to hear any final speeches, Johnny. It's not over 'til it's over."

He stopped in the middle of the path, and she walked into his back. He turned around, saying, "I just wanted you to know I love you."

She moved around him and took the lead. "I don't want to hear that, Johnny."

"Well, you heard it, whether you wanted to or not."

"Look, I'll admit there's a physical attraction—"

"It's more than that, Sandy."

"No. That's all it is. And from now on there's not even going to be that."

"Back to being the hard-bitten cop, huh?"

"Back to reality."

"There are different realities," said Johnny.

"No, that's where you're wrong. There's only one reality, Johnny. All the rest is justification or wishful thinking."

"I wasn't trying to start a philosophical discussion here, I only wanted to tell you how I felt."

"Stop it! Stop it now, Johnny. You're making me crazy."

She expected some other retort, but he fell silent behind her, and all she could hear of him after a while were his squishy footfalls behind her.

His head was aching and he had occasional double vision, but he would never admit it to her. He was bruised all over from the roof coming down on him, and he had a feeling that at least one of his ribs was broken. The walking didn't hurt them, but breathing sure as hell did.

He was having a hard time believing Chance was a crooked cop. Of all the cops he'd met, Chance was maybe the one he'd have thought least likely to go bad. Maybe that was just because he'd gotten to like him, though. You didn't want to think that about someone you liked.

He should have seen it. He should have put two and two together just by how quickly they'd been gotten to in both safe houses. He had slipped up, and he could only figure that Sandy had been the cause of that. You fall in love, you let your defenses down.

He knew what she was going through. He knew she felt the same way he did but couldn't admit it, not to herself, certainly not to him. He admired her all the more for it.

There was barking up ahead, and the dog didn't reappear on the path the way he had done before. Maybe he'd caught up with one of the other dogs. Maybe something worse. Maybe Chance was going to ambush them and finish them off.

He reached out and grabbed Sandy's arm. "Let me go ahead," he said to her.

"I'll stay in front," she said. "I have the gun."

"I have the tranquilizer gun," he said.

"What are you going to do with it, stun an alligator?"

He hadn't thought of that. He knew there were alligators in the Everglades, but it was easy to forget when you didn't see any. He wasn't even sure her .45 would do the job on an alligator. Might scare him off, but it wouldn't stop him.

The path made a turn, and they found themselves in a clearing. A bamboo hut on stilts was up ahead, and the Doberman was circling it, barking.

Just as Sandy yelled to the dog, a Seminole Indian came out of the hut and looked down at them. He wondered if this was the one who wrestled alligators.

Showing no fear of the dog, the Indian climbed down the ladder and stood, immobile, watching them.

The dog stopped barking and wriggled over to the man, putting on his damn puppy act again.

"Could you tell us how to get out of here?" Sandy asked the Indian.

"You the ones came in by helicopter?" he asked her.

Sandy nodded. "Is there some way out of here?"

"There are many ways out of here if you know them."

"Look, I'm a cop," said Sandy, but the Indian interrupted her.

"I'm glad to hear that, since you're carrying a firearm."

"It's very important that we get out of here. There's a man trying to kill us—"

The Indian held up a hand to stop her. "Being lost is enough of a reason for wanting to get out of here. You take my canoe, I take your dog."

Johnny could tell she was torn. But there was the damn dog, acting like he'd always lived with the Indian, licking the man's hand, leaning against his leg.

"It's a deal," said Johnny, "and if we can, we'll have it returned to you."

"I have many canoes, but I don't have a good dog like this."

He gave them water to drink and some crackers, then led them through the jungle to a stream. Tied up beside it was a flat-bottomed boat that didn't bear much resemblance to Johnny's idea of a canoe.

When they managed to get in without tipping it, the Indian handed them each a paddle and thanked them for the dog. The man was smiling as though he'd put something over on them, but Johnny would gladly have given him all the Dobermans and thrown in a little extra just to have a means out of the place.

The Indian pointed them in the right direction, and they started to paddle, coordinating their strokes. It was hot with the sun beating down on them, but the forward motion of the boat brought up a little breeze, and it was damn good to get off his feet.

"I know you didn't want to give up that dog," said Johnny.

"He seemed happy there."

"That dog would've made mincemeat of Jackson."

"Oh, no. You ought to see Jackson with dogs. He'd have scared him to death."

"Your cottage is rather small for a Doberman."

"I know. But I kind of got attached to him."

He liked that in her, the way she was with animals. He imagined that when she was a little girl she was the kind of child who brought home strays, or lured them home. She was loving with animals without being silly about them. He didn't imagine that Fidel got fancy haircuts or silly bows, or that she'd ever think of dressing him in a sweater, even if the Miami climate should suddenly change drastically. He could imagine her being the same with children: a caring, loving mother, but not the kind who talked baby talk and dressed them up and played with them like dolls.

He shifted into one of his favorite daydreams of late—the one where he was living with her in her cottage, sitting with her at night with a fire in the fireplace, mugs of coffee on the table in front of them, him reading a book, Sandy doing her needlepoint, both of them content with the moment but also looking forward to when they'd go to bed. He fast-forwarded the daydream a little, moving into the part where they were undressing for bed, when he heard a noise behind them and looked around.

Coming up fast was an airboat, and he didn't think there was going to be room for it to pass. And if it did pass, it was moving with such speed that it would probably tip them over.

It must have been because his mind was still on the daydream that it was Sandy who saw who it was in the airboat and yelled out, "It's Chance, Johnny—duck down!"

Instead of shots, though, the sound of the boat subsided, and he lifted his head to see it several yards behind them and keeping a steady pace.

It was Chance and he had a shotgun in his arms. When he raised it, Johnny ducked down and took out the tranquilizer gun. He didn't think it would do any good, but it made him feel better to have some kind of weapon in his hand.

Five shots were fired in quick succession, and the canoe suddenly sprouted holes in the sides and water started to come in at an alarming rate.

"We're going to have to jump for it," said Sandy, getting off a shot but missing Chance.

"Try scooping it out with your hands," said Johnny. "There're probably alligators in the water." And before she could give him any more orders, he dived over the side and swam underwater toward Chance's boat. Once underwater he was sorry he had said that about alligators. He'd never met up with one, and he didn't want this to be the day.

He could see Chance leaning over the side of the boat, waiting for him to appear. Johnny made a splash on that side, then quickly went under the boat and came up on the other side. Before Chance could see where he was, he tipped the airboat and had the satisfaction of seeing Chance go off the other side, his shotgun now lying on the bottom of the stream and useless.

Johnny swam over to Chance, who was waiting for him. He grabbed him by the throat and tried to shove his head under water, but Chance countered by kneeing him in the groin, and Johnny bent over double, his own head submerging. Chance grabbed it and held it under, and Johnny, still reeling with the pain, saw the bloody wound on Chance's leg and gave it a punch with his fist. The water prevented him from hitting with the force he wanted, but Chance let go of him and grabbed his leg.

Johnny grabbed the tranquilizer gun from his waistband and hoped it worked underwater. He got off a shot at close range before Chance saw what he was doing and grabbed it out of his hand. He tossed it away and came at Johnny again, and then they were wrestling in the water, and Chance had the advantage, because his arms were the size of Johnny's legs. Johnny kicked out at Chance's leg again, but missed, and Chance got hold of his neck. Now it was his head underwater, and he held his breath and wondered where the hell Sandy was and why she wasn't protecting him.

Just when he thought he was going to start seeing his life flash before his eyes, he felt the fingers loosen around his neck, and then he was coming to the surface and gasping for air and thanking God he hadn't drowned. It was then that he saw Sandy leaning over the airboat with her gun pressed to Chance's temple, and he realized he had her to thank once again, and not God.

"I think I ought to just shoot him," said Sandy calmly, "or he's just going to give us trouble all the way back."

Johnny had heard this bluff of hers before and didn't take it seriously until he heard the safety being released. He grabbed the makeshift bandage off his head, saying, "I'll tie up his hands."

"Never mind that," said Sandy, throwing him the rope used to tie the boat to the dock, "use this. I've got a better idea. We'll tow him in, like a whale. If he can keep his head above water he lives. If not, well, it's his funeral."

Chance was silent and deathly pale. Johnny tied his wrists together, and then tied his wrists to his ankles so that Chance resembled a frog. "I think we ought to take him in the boat," he said to Sandy. "By the looks of his leg, he's getting gangrene, and we want him to live for his trial.''

Chance let out a stream of curses, and Johnny happily gagged him with the piece of sweatshirt. He hadn't felt like putting it back around his head anyway.

Sandy turned pale when she saw Chance's leg. She didn't say anything, though, when Johnny dumped him on the bottom of the boat and took over the navigating. The airboat was more like it. They'd get to civilization ten times faster than in the canoe.

They would get there all too fast, in fact, and then they'd be separated. The thought was almost enough to make him turn around and head back. The cabin might have been miserable, but at least he'd been with Sandy.

Sandy had hardly gotten off the phone when the first squad car pulled up. They told her that an ambulance was on the way and asked whether she wanted to drive with them. She decided she wanted to go to the hospital with Chance. Until she saw him there, under guard, she wouldn't feel safe.

She was walking back to where Johnny was waiting in the office when the black sedan pulled in and two agents got out. They walked into the office and talked to Johnny for a moment, then led him out.

She looked over at Johnny, and their eyes met and held. Pride kept her from going near him. She could see he was waiting for her to make a move or say something, but she stood there, frozen. It didn't seem real that he was being taken away from her. It didn't seem real that she cared.

He finally gave her a nod, then turned and got into the back seat of the car. She watched it drive off and suddenly thought of all the things she could have said.

Sandy walked into the office where Chance, still tied up, was huddled in the corner. He gave her the look of a wild animal being attacked when she walked over to him. She reached down and took the gag out of his mouth.

"I never wanted you hurt," he said to her.

She ignored him, wishing she had the change to use the soft drink machine.

"At the end, it was your skin or mine."

"So, being chivalrous, you chose your own," she said, walking over to a chair and sitting down.

He started to say something else, but the sound of the ambulance drowned him out.

She stayed at the hospital long enough to find out that they weren't going to have to amputate Chance's leg; then she checked with hospital security and the guards on his door before asking for a ride to head-quarters.

Looking out the window of the squad car she saw the damage from the hurricane everywhere. They passed a trailer park where the trailers were all over-turned, houses with their roofs blown off, trees down everywhere, telephone lines across flattened parked cars, and children out playing everywhere, which must mean the schools had been closed.

"How bad was the damage overall?" she asked the driver.

"Not as bad as they expected," he said. "The hurricane had lost a lot of its force by the time it hit land."

"Miami Beach?"

"Lots of broken glass and uprooted palm trees. The worst hit were the boats that didn't get out of the Intracoastal in time. Quite a few fires, but nothing monumental. Where were you?"

"In the middle of the Everglades."

He nodded. "You were lucky. That was probably the safest place to be."

Chapter 12

Y̶ou look like hell, McGee."

"Yes, sir."

Lieutenant Wainger shook his head and started being overprotective again. "Sit down. You look like you're going to collapse."

Sandy stood up straighter. If she sat down she might never get up again.

"That was an order, McGee."

Sandy removed the handgun from the waistband of her shorts and placed it on his desk. "I'm quitting, Lieutenant."

She saw that she now had his full attention. "That's a natural reaction, McGee, but you'll get over it."

"I don't think so, sir."

The lieutenant got up from behind his desk, walked over to the door and closed it, then held out a chair for her. She sat down on the edge of the chair so her feet touched the floor, but she didn't relax.

"I've been thinking about that request you made to me a couple of months ago, McGee, about wanting to go undercover. That still interest you?"

"No."

"McGee, you're one of my best cops. You just went through a rough few days, but you came out of it looking like a hero."

"I don't want to be a hero. I want to go home, Lieutenant."

"Of course you do. Listen, take some vacation time, think it over."

Sandy shook her head and stood. "I'm not changing my mind," she said.

When he didn't argue she left his office and went over to her desk. She should clean it out, take her stuff home. She didn't think she wanted any of it, though. She didn't think she wanted anything that reminded her of the job. She knew she didn't want anything that reminded her of Chance.

A tree was down in her front yard. It was her largest tree, the one that shaded the front windows. She guessed she was lucky it had fallen away from the house and not on top of it. She'd have to call the owner and see about getting it hauled away.

She walked around to the back and found it a shambles. Her patio furniture had been blown all over the yard, and the hammock had disappeared. The windows were intact, though, which meant the rain hadn't gotten in the house.

She let herself in the back door, and it was several seconds before Fidel came out of the bedroom. His tail was going, but he looked spooked. She picked him up and held him for a minute, then got out food for both animals and put it down for them. There was no sign of Jackson, but then she heard a faint cry, and he came squeezing out from behind the refrigerator.

She opened a window and turned up the air conditioner, then stripped in the kitchen and threw everything she was wearing in the trash. She thought of the clothes she had left at Turnberry and wondered if she'd ever get them back. It would necessitate a call to the lieutenant, and she didn't want to talk to him again.

She washed her hair three times in the shower and then stood under the hot water until she started to feel clean again. She thought of the last time she had stood under this shower. Johnny and Chance had been out in the kitchen, and she'd been looking forward to buying them some clothes. She'd have to make up an expense sheet for the lieutenant and get reimbursed. Or maybe she'd forget about that, too.

She fixed herself some hot tea and a couple of slices of toast, then left the dishes in the sink and went to bed. This was what she had been looking forward to, being in her own bed, safe and dry, but she couldn't stop thinking about Johnny. She wondered if she'd ever stop thinking about Johnny.

They were back in the jungle, dodging the bullets from Chance's gun. They couldn't see where the shots were coming from, and the Doberman was going crazy, running around in circles, and Sandy was shooting wildly every time she saw something move.

She felt someone grab her by the shoulder, and she tried to shake them off, afraid it was Chance, but then she heard Annie's voice and wondered how she had gotten here.

"Wake up, Sandy."

Sandy opened her eyes, but for a moment the dream seemed more real than the reality.

"When did you get back?"

"Annie."

"The one and only. Where were you when the hurricane struck? I was worried about you."

Sandy pushed herself up and put a pillow behind her head. "In the middle of the Everglades."

"I guess that was a pretty good place to be."

"It was a nightmare," said Sandy.

"You okay, honey?" asked Annie, sitting down on the bed beside her.

"No," said Sandy, shaking her head and hoping she wouldn't cry. Annie and Bolivia never cried, and she'd learned not to, too. Only she felt so miserable it would feel good to cry.

"You want to talk about it?"

Sandy shook her head, then started talking anyway. She told her about Chance and how he'd tried to kill them and how he was in the hospital and almost had to have his leg amputated.

"*Chance?*"

Sandy nodded.

"And here I was hoping . . ."

"I liked him, too. Not that way, but we were getting along really well. I thought we were all looking out for each other, and all the time he was the one setting us up."

"That's rough. Your own partner."

"And Johnny...oh, God, Annie, I fell in love with him."

"It was bound to happen, all three of you in danger like that. You'll get over it."

"Are you sure?"

"Sandy, you couldn't love a bad cop."

"I know, but I do."

"You didn't—"

"No, we were never really alone together."

"Well, that's good, anyway."

Sandy wasn't so sure. More than anything she would have liked to make love with him. "I don't understand it, Annie. He's not the kind of person you'd believe it of. He was a good person, I'd swear."

"Would you have believed it of Chance?"

Sandy shook her head.

"All kinds go bad, Sandy. I saw it when I was a prosecutor."

"He was so good to me. He talked me to sleep and then held me off the floor, out of the water."

"Are you sure he's a bad cop?"

"Of course I'm sure. That's why he needed protection."

"Will you be testifying against Chance?"

"I don't know. I quit my job, Annie."

"Oh, no, Sandy, you didn't really, did you?"

"I handed in my gun and quit. The lieutenant told me to take some vacation time and think it over, but I don't have to think it over."

"You'll change your mind. You're too good a cop to quit."

"I hate it."

"I don't blame you after the experience you just went through, but you'll forget about it."

"I don't like being a cop, Annie. I've never really liked it."

"What else would you do?"

"I don't know. But I'll tell you something, I'd rather sell clothes in Burdine's than ever go back."

"Get dressed and come home with me, Sandy. Have dinner with us. You shouldn't be here all alone after what you've been through."

"Thanks, Annie, but I'd really rather stay home."

"Come on, you probably don't even have any food in the house."

"I always have food in the house."

"I've missed seeing you."

"Not tonight, Annie. All I want to do is stay in bed and be with my animals. Did I tell you about the Doberman?"

"You told me."

"How am I going to forget about him, Annie?"

"You ought to start going out, Sandy. I know a lot of lawyers I can fix you up with, and Jack knows professors."

"I don't want to date."

Annie suddenly brightened. "Did I tell you Bolivia called?"

"No. When was that?"

"In the middle of the night. I accused her of not being able to figure out the time difference, but she said it was the only time she was sure of getting me."

"Is she okay?"

"She says it's great. The beaches are never crowded."

Sandy started to smile. "That sounds just like her."

"She says they don't get hurricanes in Lebanon."

"No, they just get bombed," said Sandy, then remembered she had recently been bombed, too.

"Guess what?"

"What?"

"She and Tooley got married."

"I don't believe it."

"Well, they got married over there, so I'm not sure how legal it is, but she said he insisted on it."

"I can't picture Bolivia married."

"Well, I'm sure it's not your average marriage."

"It's all happened so fast. Last spring we were all single."

"I always thought you'd be the first to get married," said Annie.

"I was the only one who wanted to."

"I mean it, I'm going to start fixing you up."

"Give me a little time, Annie, okay?"

"I'll give you two weeks, Sandy, and then get ready to rejoin society."

Sandy was afraid two weeks wouldn't even begin to do it.

* * *

On Sunday she looked at the classified ads in the *Times*. The only kind of job there for ex-cops were security jobs, and she didn't want to do that. Anything else, though, she wasn't qualified for. She couldn't type; she had no sales experience; she'd never even worked as a waitress. She had enough money to live on for a couple of months, and she wondered whether she ought to learn word processing. She wondered if she'd have to be able to type in order to do it.

Out of boredom she read the entire classified section, and when she came to the Pets for Sale, she saw someone advertising Doberman pinschers. The last thing she needed was another dog, especially a very large dog, but she didn't have anything else to do, so she called the number in the paper, and a man gave her directions on how to get there.

She drove down to Homestead and found he lived out in the country on several acres. And he wasn't just selling off a single litter of puppies, he bred them.

His name was Al Jackson, and she told him she had a cat named Jackson, and he asked her if she was looking for a puppy. She ended up telling him about the FBI's Dobermans.

"So one went bad," he said.

"You mean the friendly one?"

He nodded. "He didn't take the training well."

"He was my favorite."

"I train them for security here, but I don't like to do it. They start out friendly puppies, and you turn them into killers. That's what people want Dobermans for, though. They want guard dogs."

"Is it hard to breed dogs?"

"You get a male and a female, and then they take it from there."

"Can you support yourself on it?"

"Oh, yes. It was slow at first, but I'm doing well now. You interested in breeding dogs?"

"I think I'd like to."

"You ought to try it with one of those fancy little dogs, the ones that are so popular now."

"I don't like them."

"No, neither do I. Well, Dobermans are always in demand. You decide to do it, come on by and I'll teach you what I've learned so far."

She drove home with a plan forming in her mind.

Sandy jumped every time the phone rang. She knew he wasn't going to call her, but she couldn't keep from hoping. It wasn't that she'd changed her mind about him, but she kept wishing they could have said goodbye. The way he'd just walked off like that with neither of them saying anything, it didn't seem like the right ending. In fact, it didn't seem like an ending at all. She felt she had to say goodbye to him before it would really be over.

This time, though, it was the lieutenant.

"Changed your mind yet?" he asked her.

"No, sir."

"Well, that's not what I called about. You hear about Madrigal?"

She hadn't heard because she hadn't been reading the papers. The police corruption trial had started, and she was avoiding the papers and the television news because she was afraid that if she read about Johnny, or, worse, saw him on television, she'd be lost.

"He's singing," said the lieutenant.

"I'm not surprised," said Sandy.

"Thanks to him, I think we've finally got a case against Rivera."

"That's who he worked for?"

"That's Madrigal, he goes right to the top."

"What's going to happen to him?"

There was silence on the other end.

"You didn't make a deal with him, did you?"

"You know the way it works, McGee."

"He's getting immunity?"

"We're going to put Rivera away this time."

"But he tried to kill me!"

"You know how it is, McGee."

"But it shouldn't be that way."

"If you're worried he's going to come after you—"

"Of course I'm not worried about that. I just don't think it's right, that's all."

"Not much in life is, McGee."

The following Friday she went over to Annie's for dinner. Annie and Jack lived in a lovely old Spanish home in Coral Gables that Sandy was crazy about. All the way over she was worried that Annie might have invited some single man over for her, in which case she was going to leave as soon as she was finished eating. It turned out to be just Annie and Jack, though, and she relaxed.

It wasn't raining for a change, and they ate outside on the terrace and watched the sun set over the canal. The conversation had been general, with Annie and Jack doing most of the talking, but after Annie brought the dessert out she said, "Have you decided what you're going to do, Sandy?"

"I've been thinking about it," she said.

"Have you come up with anything?"

"You have to promise not to laugh."

"Well, now that you've said that, I'm sure to laugh," said Annie, already starting to smile.

"Ignore her," said Jack. "I won't laugh."

"I'm thinking of breeding Dobermans."

"Beautiful dogs," said Jack.

"That's the most ridiculous thing I ever heard," said Annie, but at least she wasn't laughing.

"I've decided I like animals better than people."

"Oh, Sandy," said Annie, "just because you had one bad experience with a man, you can't give up on people."

"I'm tired of always having to deal with cops and criminals. I want something else, Annie. And you know I love animals."

"You can always do it as a hobby. Why not breed some of those long-haired cats that go for so much? I don't see where you'd even have room for Dobermans over there. Your yard's not that big."

"I'm thinking of moving to Arizona."

Annie got very still.

"I can't stand the rain," said Sandy, hoping that Annie would understand. "The rain depresses me. I'd like to live somewhere where the sun is always out and everything is dry."

"That sounds like the desert," said Jack.

She nodded.

"I'm getting kind of tired of all this rain, too," said Jack. "You've got to admit, though, we have gorgeous winters."

"Oh, Sandy, I'd just hate it if you moved that far away. I'd never see you."

"You could come out and visit."

"It wouldn't be the same."

Sandy knew it wouldn't be the same. But it wasn't the same with Annie married and Bolivia off in Lebanon, either. She knew that one of these days Jack and Annie would start having children; she didn't think Bolivia and Tooley would ever return to the States. It was just going to be her, all alone, and she might as well be alone somewhere else.

And every time it rained it reminded her of Chance and Johnny. Maybe if she got far enough away she'd forget about him.

It was Saturday night, and Annie and Jack had invited her to a party they were going to, but she wanted to stay home. It was raining again and had been for days. Another hurricane had swept by, this time too far out to do any damage, bringing torrential rains.

It was a waste of good energy, and it made her feel a little guilty, but she turned the air conditioner to high and lit a fire in the fireplace. She thought it might be the only way to get the sticky feeling out of the house. Nothing ever seemed to get really dry anymore.

She got into her pink flannel robe, brewed herself a pot of tea and curled up on the couch to work on some needlepoint. Jackson was in front of the fireplace, as close to the screen as he could manage to get. Fidel was beside her on the couch.

She could hear the rain pounding down on the roof, and it reminded her of the cabin. She knew her roof wasn't going to cave in, but the sound depressed her. She finally got up and put some music on, vintage Rolling Stones. If that couldn't lift her depression, nothing could.

At first she thought it was a branch that had been blown against the house, but when Fidel jumped off the couch and ran to the front door, she knew someone was knocking. She hoped it wasn't Annie and Jack trying to change her mind about the party. Even if she felt like a party, the last thing she felt like was going out in the rain.

The knock came again, and she set down her needlepoint and got up to answer it.

She thought she recognized him through the glass in the door, but it seemed more likely that her mind and the rain streaming down the glass were playing tricks on her.

She opened the door, and he stood there, soaking wet, and she could see he was a little afraid.

"Johnny."

"May I come in?"

She should have slammed the door in his face, but she wouldn't do that to anyone who was soaked to the skin and asking for shelter. She stood aside and let him enter. He stood for a moment on the area rug, letting some of the water drip off him.

"You're soaked."

"I'm getting used to it."

"Take your shoes off, Johnny, and go in front of the fire."

He looked into the living room then, and she saw his eyes go to the fire, then to her pot of tea on the coffee table, and then to her needlepoint, where they rested for a moment.

"It's just the way I pictured it," he said.

"Well, you've been here before."

He walked over to the fire, and she went to the linen closet, returning with a blanket. She handed it to him saying, "You might as well get out of those wet clothes. I can put them in the dryer for you. Can I get you a drink?"

"How about a cup of coffee?"

She went out to the kitchen and gave him time to get out of his clothes. When she returned he was seated on the other end of the couch with Fidel in his lap. She gathered his wet clothes and carried them to the dryer. They should only take about twenty minutes, but that would give him enough time to say what he had to say. Then she'd ask him to leave, and it would be final this time. But, oh, it was so good to see him.

"How're you doing?" he asked her.

"I quit the force."

"I'm not surprised," he said.

"Everyone else was."

"But they didn't go through what we did."

"Should you be here?" she asked him, not even knowing if the trial was over yet.

"I think so. What do you think?"

She didn't know what to say to that. She picked up her needlepoint but could no longer remember how to do it, and set it down again.

"Did you follow the trial?" he asked her.

"No."

"Not at all?"

"I've been avoiding the news. The lieutenant told me about Chance giving evidence, but that's all."

"Then you don't know about me."

She looked at him. "What about you?"

"I wasn't a cop, Sandy."

"What do you mean?"

"I was FBI. Undercover."

"Undercover?" she asked, realizing what that meant but not able to believe it yet.

"You don't know how many times I wanted to tell you."

"But you didn't trust me."

"Most of the time I did. But it's just as well I didn't, because I had an urge to tell Chance, too."

"I wondered," she said.

"You wondered what?"

"I wondered how I could be attracted to a bad cop."

"I know. I knew it was eating at you."

He put his arm around the back of the couch, and she moved over close to him. She wondered what all of this meant. "I don't like the Feds," she said.

"I remember."

"I don't mean I'd rather you were a bad cop."

"I know."

"Will they try to kill you?"

"What for? I wasn't one of them."

"Will you be able to go undercover again?"

"No."

"Oh."

"Because I quit."

She looked at him, and he was smiling. And then he gently lifted Fidel off his lap and put him on the floor, and before Fidel could jump up again, Johnny had taken her in his arms and there was no more room for a small dog because their bodies were pressed together.

He wasn't a bad cop, he wasn't even FBI anymore, he was just Johnny, and he'd come to her. Their mouths met, and she no longer minded the sound of the rain on the roof, she loved it. She and Johnny were together inside, so what did it matter if it never stopped raining?

She wanted the kiss to go on forever, but at the same time she had to ask him something. She broke off the kiss but stayed in his arms. "What's your name?" she asked him.

"Random. John Random."

"I love that name. It's a great name."

He smiled. "Anything else you want to know?"

"Are you really from Indiana? Was that story about your dog the truth?"

"All true," he said.

"How old are you?"

"Does it matter?"

"No." And it didn't; nothing mattered.

"Thirty."

"So am I," she said.

"I don't believe it."

"Don't start, Johnny. No talk of midgets or how old I look."

"I wouldn't think of it. I don't even know why we're talking."

"Couldn't we talk for a while? Get to know each other before—"

"Before what?"

"Before we go to bed."

"I guess we could do that," said Johnny, shifting so that she was on his lap and he was looking down at her.

"What're you going to do now?" she asked him.

"I haven't really thought about it. All I thought about was seeing you again and asking you to marry me. That is, if you love me. I thought you did at the time, but when I didn't see you, I began to have doubts."

"I love you so much it frightens me."

"It doesn't frighten me at all," he said, looking very pleased.

"I've been thinking of moving to Arizona," she told him. "To raise Dobermans."

"Tired of the rain?"

"Very tired."

"That sounds good to me. Maybe we could have some horses, too."

"You know anything about horses?"

"No. You know anything about Dobermans?"

"Not really," said Sandy.

"Then we'll start from scratch."

"Okay," said Sandy. "I think we've done enough talking."

"Do you?"

"Oh, yes."

"I've fantasized this moment so much that now..."

"Me too," she said, "but I always stopped at the part where we got into bed."

"I didn't stop there," said Johnny.

"You didn't?"

"Why would I want to stop there?"

He pulled her close to him and stood up in one effortless move. The blanket that he had been wrapped in fell to the floor, and she felt overdressed in her robe against his naked body. And then he was heading for her bedroom, and for once she didn't mind feeling small; she felt loved and protected and very much like a woman, not a child.

She put her arms around his neck and nestled her head against his chest. He held her with one arm as he took off her furry slippers and dropped them on the floor. "Now my robe," she murmured, and heard his low chuckle.

"Still trying to give me orders?" he asked her.

"Now my robe, please," she amended.

Once in her bedroom, he lowered her to her feet and turned on a small lamp. By the time the light reached her, she was out of her robe.

He reached out for her, and then they were tumbling onto her bed, lips meeting, legs tangling, hands exploring, and bodies catching fire. When at last he entered her, she was oblivious to the rain pounding against the windows and the cat perched on the dresser and Fidel making woofing sounds from the doorway. She was held captive by the sweet, consuming heat and the chain reaction going off inside her body. She could hear herself cry out as the final nova burst into light before fading.

With awareness came a calm contentment. When she finally managed to speak, it was, "Well," and it sounded more like a sigh of satisfaction than anything else.

"Yes," he agreed, still holding on to her tightly.

"Oh, my," said Sandy, more shaken than she had ever thought possible.

"Was it anything like your fantasy?" she asked him, wanting his approval but very much hating to ask for it.

"It didn't even come close," he said.

Sandy was silent for a very long moment. "Am I to understand that to mean that your fantasy was better?" She couldn't keep a slight trace of annoyance out of her voice.

He laughed somewhat breathlessly. "No. Oh, no. In no way," he assured her.

"No?"

"Do I have to tell you what that was like?"

"Well, no, I guess not," said Sandy.

"Incredible," said Johnny, rolling off her and pulling her close.

"It *was* incredible," said Sandy, feeling awed at what two bodies had wrought.

"It was more than incredible," said Johnny. "It was stupefying."

Sandy thought about that for a moment. "I don't much like the sound of that word," she said.

"Superhuman," said Johnny, really getting into it.

"Well..."

"On a scale of one to ten, I'd give it a fifteen," he said, his mouth moving down to her neck and pausing there.

"Do we really have to grade it?" asked Sandy.

"Not really. Is there something you'd rather do?" His lips moved from her neck and traveled slowly down to one breast.

"No, no, just keep on with what you're doing," she said, wondering if it was even remotely possible that they could achieve a twenty.

* * * * *

COMING
NEXT MONTH

#337 RUNAWAY—Emilie Richards

With the help of journalist Jess Cantrell, Kristin Jensen posed as a prostitute to find her missing sister. Despite the constant danger, she found herself attracted to Jess. Was it purely physical . . . or could Kristin's hazardous search be leading to a safe haven of love?

#338 NOT WITHOUT HONOR—
Marilyn Pappano

Held hostage as a political pawn in a steamy South American rebel camp, Brenna Mathis, daughter of a military advisor, discovered that Andrés Montano, leader of the rebel forces and her former lover, had masterminded her abduction! Could the man she'd once loved still be the captor of her heart?

#339 IGUANA BAY—Theresa Weir

Elise Ramsey had been kidnapped—twice in one week! The first man wanted to use her as an alibi at his murder trial. The second, ruggedly handsome bounty hunter Dylan Davis, wanted to prevent her from testifying. To make matters even worse, Elise realized she was falling in love with this madman!

#340 FOREVER MY LOVE—
Heather Graham Pozzessere

Brent McQueen and his ex-wife Kathy were thrown together unexpectedly when smugglers mistakenly believed he had information they needed. Chased by killers and racing to uncover the truth before it was too late, they found passion flaring anew as they discovered that a love like theirs was, indeed, meant to last forever.

You'll flip . . . your pages won't!
Read paperbacks *hands-free* with

Book Mate · I

The perfect "mate" for all your romance paperbacks

Traveling · Vacationing · At Work · In Bed · Studying · Cooking · Eating

Perfect size for all standard paperbacks, this wonderful invention makes reading a pure pleasure! Ingenious design holds paperback books OPEN and FLAT so even wind can't ruffle pages – leaves your hands free to do other things. Reinforced, wipe-clean vinyl-covered holder flexes to let you turn pages without undoing the strap . . . supports paperbacks so well, they have the strength of hardcovers!

Pages turn WITHOUT opening the strap

SEE-THROUGH STRAP

Reinforced back stays flat

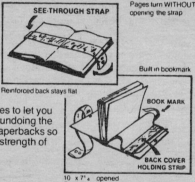

Built in bookmark

BOOK MARK

BACK COVER HOLDING STRIP

10 x 7'₄ opened
Snaps closed for easy carrying too

Available now. Send your name, address, and zip code, along with a check or money order for just $5.95 + .75¢ for postage & handling (for a total of $6.70) payable to Reader Service to:

Reader Service
Bookmate Offer
901 Fuhrmann Blvd.
P.O. Box 1396
Buffalo, N.Y. 14269-1396

Offer not available in Canada
*New York and Iowa residents add appropriate sales tax.

BM-G

Silhouette Intimate Moments®

**Beginning next month,
Intimate Moments will bring you
two gripping stories by Emilie Richards**

Coming in June
Runaway
by EMILIE RICHARDS
Intimate Moments #337

Coming in July
The Way Back Home
by EMILIE RICHARDS
Intimate Moments #341

Krista and Rosie Jensen were two sisters who had it all—
until a painful secret tore them apart.

They were two special women who met two very special men
who made life a little easier—and love a whole lot better—
until the day when Krista and Rosie could be sisters once
again.

You'll laugh, you'll cry and you'll never, ever forget. Don't
miss the first book, RUNAWAY, available next month at your
favorite retail outlet.

Silhouette Books®

A BIG SISTER
can take her places

She likes that. Her Mom does too.

BIG BROTHERS/BIG SISTERS AND HARLEQUIN

Harlequin is proud to announce its official sponsorship of Big Brothers/Big Sisters of America. Look for this poster in your local Big Brothers/Big Sisters agency or call them to get one in your favorite bookstore. Love is all about sharing.